Al Williams   Bruce King
   | |
Cynthia Gene Janet
         age

Lynn — Hunter — Janet / Edward
                                   8 yrs
                                (short)

Joan Pierce
    |
  Jane

Carrie — Johnnie.

Are you my Father?

Margo Walter

Are You My Father? is a work of fiction. Names, characters, places, and incidents are the products of the author's imagination or are used fictitiously. Any resemblance to actual events, locations, or persons, living or dead, is entirely coincidental.

Are You My Father?
© 2020 by Margo Walter

All rights reserved. This book or any portion thereof may not be reproduced or used in any manner whatsoever without the express written permission of the publisher except for the use of brief quotations in a book review.

ISBN (Print): 978-1-09833-653-0
ISBN (eBook): 978-1-09833-654-7

This story would not have been possible without the love and support of my son, Will, and my daughter, Nicole.
May your roads through life be adventuresome and productive.
Help each other with your challenges and share the good times and happy celebrations with each other.
You are my *raison d'etre* and I love you both with all my heart.

Contents

Prologue	1
Chapter 1: Out of the Nest	3
Chapter 2: Afraid to Fly	9
Chapter 3: Learning to Fly	72
Chapter 4: Spreading My Wings	90
Chapter 5: Learning to Fly Straight	111
Chapter 6: Surviving	163
Chapter 7: Letting Go	179
Chapter 8: The Secret Is Out	181
Chapter 9: My Nest	184
Chapter 10: I Am Responsible	189
Chapter 11: Learning to Soar	195
Chapter 12: Practicing an Attitude of Gratitude	211
Chapter 13: Soaring like an Eagle	219
Epilogue	226

Prologue

With the present parenting options, it is no longer true that you cannot choose your parents. It is more accurate to say that your parents can be selected for you. Sperm banks, artificial insemination, open adoptions, closed adoptions, surrogacy, harvesting of embryos, and yes, cloning—which is on the cusp of scientific inquiry—create opportunities for producing babies, which was assumed to be impossible.

Let me stop you right there. This story is about a well-known method of conception that also has lots of names: getting knocked up, having a casual affair, entrapping a man by getting pregnant, not practicing safe sex. P. D. Eastman wrote a book for the Doctor Seuss series called *Are You My Mother?* The story is about a bird who falls out of his nest, loses the protection of his home, and sets out to find his mother. The little fledgling bird travels many roads to find his mother. The story takes him to numerous parts of the world, and he runs into many roadblocks. The journey also exposes him to a variety of different creatures in his own neighborhood. He is always asking the question, "Are you my mother?"

This narrative is a search for the truth and asks the question, "Are you my father?" Through the adversities of life, I also lost the comfort, safety, and security of my nest. However, my persistence and my life experiences—good, bad, ugly, mysterious, and miraculous—help me to answer the essential questions and find the safety and happiness that most of us seek. My roadblocks do turn into stepping-stones.

Feelings, emotions, and behaviors are ever-changing. This story could be your own as you travel your roads to life. It has taken years of introspection, countless hours of therapy, and the ability to assemble puzzles to create this story. There was a deliberate stalling on my part until certain family members died.

Different adventures do occur with house moves, job changes, personal relationships, and life and death experiences that most of us encounter with our own itinerary. Everyone takes a different direction, and one turn can affect the outcome of that trip. I am no exception. Hang on as I take you on my life journey, and you might then look back on your own.

Chapter 1: Out of the Nest

There are five chairs lined up in a perfect row. Everything is set up in an ideal way. There are white folding chairs on a red rug surrounded by a beautifully maintained green lawn with white headstones as far as you can see. Every so often, a large tombstone sticks its head out of the ground, and you can spot at least one mausoleum in the distance. There is a slight breeze, but the humidity is hanging over the crowd. No one is speaking, and almost everyone is wearing black, as expected. There are ten men dressed in military uniforms, three with swords and seven with rifles. Everyone next to me and standing in front of me, including the pallbearers, is sweating profusely. July in the nation's capital is sweltering, and humid and this day is no exception. As a rule, I do not sweat profusely. However, my dress is sticking to my body. There is that yucky feeling when you are so hot that the back of your neck begs for a cold washcloth or a couple of ice cubes. Why did I spray my hair this morning? The hair spray is melting like hot honey and caking on my forehead. My husband has a band of perspiration across his forehead which he keeps wiping away with the overused tissue. Beads of sweat gather around the necklace I am wearing. It is a dull gold chain with a precious, shining heart given to me by my husband. I look at it and remember that I am loved and, My God, it is hot!!

The heels of my shoes sink into the grass, which is saturated from sprinklers that did their job before our arrival. *Why aren't I wearing flat shoes*—not only to avoid the wet turf, but to be more comfortable? I hate these black shoes and vow to trash them as soon as possible.

The 400,000 small white crosses covering 620 acres of carefully manicured lawns make quite an impression. It is my first time attending a military burial at Arlington Cemetery. Pomp and ceremony take on a new meaning. There are even horses. They are not as big as Clydesdales, but close. I am sure that underneath all that hair, the heat is most uncomfortable. One horse breaks the silence with his gentle neighing, which sounds like an intermittently working circulating fan. Six Navy men take a step forward and fire their guns as the Blue Angel jets fly overhead. That is a surprise. I know those planes show up at football games or parades, but funerals? I jump out of my skin as someone suddenly taps me on my right shoulder. The priest opens his mouth, but I do not hear any sound coming out. It all takes place in a corner of my mind that is not in the moment, except for the wet grass and giant horses. There is that surreal feeling of knowing that it is happening, but not feeling like I am a participant. I am an observer. I feel like I am standing in the shadows, but there is no shade. No, there is not even a chair for me. The other four daughters and son sit in seats of honor for our father, the Admiral.

I found my father and lost him on that miserable muggy day in Washington, DC. As I viewed the acres of white crosses, I do not remember thinking of the thousands of soldiers who were dead and buried there. I was too self-absorbed to acknowledge their presence. These men died serving their country. What about their souls? What about their afterlife?

I do believe in a Higher Power, whom I call God, but Heaven or Hell are not in my vocabulary. My spiritual journey tells me that these men did not die in vain. Their lives, just like my father's, touch all of us—the survivors. I remember what my father told me. "You only have to die once." Maybe our bodies do get buried, and our souls pass on to the universe to further influence the lives and destinies of others. My father's legacy touched so many. This funeral cannot be the end. While I do not believe in reincarnation, I know the "spirit" is mystical and transcends. My spiritual experience tells me that this funeral is not an event, but it is a process that continues beyond my father's grave. The family secret will be revealed, and others will be affected. This memorial service is definitely a new beginning in my life.

My one sister, Lynn, knows the truth. Of course, Chris, my husband, is aware of the circumstances leading up to this moment. No one understands how I feel or what made me show up at this memorial service. There were no tears, but lots of sadness. In fact, I held back all my emotions, which I learned to do at an incredibly young age. "Don't smile! Keep your lips perfectly horizontal across your face." My facial appearance is kind of a smirk, but a little more mysterious than that. I guess some people would call it the deadpan look.

I talk to no one, but there is a great deal of resentment. I am still thinking to myself: "Are you my father?" I am trying to make sense out of the events that led to this overwhelming sense of loss. Grief is where love and pain converge. "What brought me to this place in time? Who am I that I question everything and everybody?" This self-appraisal might help explain my future actions and reactions.

Most people would describe me as having an outgoing personality (the look helped with the performance), somewhat eccentric at times, a perfectionist, and sometimes compulsive. There was the time when I decided to get a llama and thirty goats one morning as I drank my morning coffee because I wanted to see if I liked being a goat herder. Middle-aged and slightly overweight, I am average-built, smart, and emotionally challenged, and can be extremely moody. Of course, these are very middle-of-the-road descriptions, and perhaps more adjectives will help define middle.

If you just hit age fifty, the "middle" moves up to age sixty, but I would still describe myself as middle-aged and one who missed my youth. However, I now qualify for those super-senior discounts at IHOP (International House of Pancakes.) Overweight? Since childhood, sermons on being "too fat" have been part of the parental communication which did nothing to help with the extra pounds. On the contrary, the constant harassing, belittling, and judging did nothing to support a ten-year-old girl lose weight. However, in high school, I did shed all those extra pounds and went straight for anorexia without passing go. Over the years, the two extremes have balanced out, and I am somewhere between too thin and preferred weight chart tables. In adulthood, I have discovered most of my friends have an extreme body-image distortion of how they look. My two athletic buddies (one bikes over fifty miles a week and the other is in the local gym five to six days a week) are constantly on diets and complaining about how fat they are becoming in old age. On the contrary, both are extremely healthy and have BMIs that anyone would be proud about. Go figure!

When I tell you that I am intelligent, I mean highly intelligent. I am not relying on my test scores but more on my creativity, my search for truths, and being a walking sponge when it comes to learning—I listen intently to everyone and everything. This is a gift and my children have been the beneficiaries.

Born with brown eyes and short blond hair (dirty blond) describes me. My intense interest in other people leads me on numerous adventures to help persons less fortunate than myself. I am an extremely caring person. I heard a college adviser say, "If we could all select a good friend, Janet would be high on the list. She has the 'good' attributes as well as the 'kinky,' which makes her fun to be around." I don't know I believed my English professor at that time, but I never forgot what she had said.

Often, I forget to look out for myself and overdo physically. I take items on my "to do" list very seriously and usually complete it all before stopping. The muscles, nerves, and bones are not what they used to be, and some chores take twice as long to accomplish than they did in the past, or in my thirties. Of course, the next day is when I pay the piper. Getting out of bed is agonizing and walking across the rug takes an incredibly long time. I am usually helpless and somewhat hopeless on the day after a hard workout. It is a struggle to keep balance in my life, physically, mentally, and emotionally. "Isn't that what shrinks are for?"

Take off the social mask, and I describe myself quite differently. From the inside-out, I am very insecure, am twenty-five pounds overweight in all the wrong places, have short and thin, lifeless hair, and have just average intelligence. I do have excessive mood swings and a host of other diagnoses that doctors have given to me over the years, which might explain the eccentricity. Loneliness is one feeling that never leaves me, and that is why I like to be around people. However, being around people does not always help my overwhelming feeling of being all alone in this world. I often feel isolated in a crowd and often perform, so others believe that I not only fit in but am also enjoying the group that I am with. It is also why I volunteer for far-out projects and get involved with the community disasters. My intelligence is overrated, and I just try to do the best possible. I cannot stand to be bored and can be somewhat of a rabble-rouser when the event calls for commitment. I do know lots and lots of people in different walks of life, but I am only genuinely close to my husband, Chris, and my children, George, David, and Kate. In fact, that is what this story is all about. *Will the real Janet Williams please stand up?*

* * *

The funeral service is breaking up. Chris and I stand aside to let others go to the car procession heading for the Omni hotel reception. Let's look at my past and maybe we can comprehend the future. What comes to mind is a reading from a little tan book called *Daily Reflections* (Alcoholics Anonymous World Services Inc., 2005, p. 36):

"What a gift it is for me to realize that all those seemingly useless years were not wasted. The most degrading and humiliating experiences turn out to be the most powerful tools in helping others to recover. In knowing the depths of shame and despair, I can reach out with a loving and compassionate hand and know that the grace of God is available to me."

Chapter 2: Afraid to Fly

Growing up in an alcoholic home, you miss your childhood altogether. You become very independent at a young age. Depending on your gender and position in the family, you take on different roles, which helps the dysfunctional family function. Family secrets become particularly important and everyone swears to secrecy. "When did I fall out of the nest?" It was before I could fly. It is imperative that I tell my story with as much honesty and truthfulness as possible.

* * *

The street was lonely when our family moved in. There were a couple of kids my age, but they were strange, nerdy, as they used to say, and had peculiar parents. At that time, I did not see my parents as weird, just absent. They would spend all their time at work and upstairs on the third floor of the house where the children were not allowed to go.

From an incredibly young age, I knew that I was different. I liked to do "risky" things and was so starved for attention that I began hurting myself at an early age to get noticed by my family members and caretakers. Nothing too serious. I would scrape my knee or bump my head. It usually worked for a short time and took the spotlight off my father, who demanded everyone's undivided attention, and my younger brother and sister, who were just too cute. The only time I was in cahoots with my siblings was when we used to hide under the dining room table or the ping-pong table and try not to breathe very loudly so no one would find us. You see, my father was very violent when he drank, and very scary. Fortunately, things changed, and there were "beautiful days in the neighborhood," as Mr. Rogers used to say.

I was out with my favorite friend, my eighty-pound German Shepherd, Duke. His fur was very black, and he only had a couple of brown spots on him that were the same color as my mother's mink coat. She wore that long furry thing when she went out partying with my father. It smelled like a dead animal or a wet cat. In any case, Duke was not just a dog. I talked to him incessantly and believed that he understood every word. I am not crazy and know that he did not talk back. However, hugging him was magical. If I was anxious, fearful, or lonely, he gave me such solace, just like every dog in my future was able to do. I learned at a young age about therapy dogs, but it took thirty-five years to comprehend and train a dog for that purpose.

Duke and I were out perusing the block of houses on our street and met this man cutting the front yard of a run-down home halfway up the block from our house. The grass was at least three feet tall (almost taller than me), the front windows were boarded up, and there was a pile of wood in the carport. The lumber looked much older than I was and was thrown all over the cement porch. Nails were sticking out of some of the boards, and it was a big mess. I was extremely nervous but decided to give this stranger, who was wearing Bermuda shorts, a top-notch interview and get the scoop. At this time, my hair was the color of the sun and went at least fifty different directions. At age five, I did look like a little "tomboy" or a waif from a shelter. My boldness overtook my fear, and I posed the first and most important question: "Do you have any kids?" It turns out that he was moving from Richmond and had three kids, an older boy, a girl one year older than me, and one girl just one year younger than I was. I told him all about everyone who lived on the street, including the Hambroughs. Those were the two nerdy girls about my age who would not even ring doorbells and run away. I liked to do superman feats and jump out of tall buildings (just a two-story built next door), and they would not even jump off the second floor onto a sand pile.

Back to the new neighbor. I just knew that he was a good guy because he started petting Duke immediately and my dog was wagging his tail profusely. There was a lot of work to be done on his house before anyone could move in. Mr. Pierce showed up every day that week to repair windows, paint walls, patch the roof, haul away rotten wood, and answer all my questions, even the silent question: "Are you my father?" I knew he wasn't, but I wished he were. It was silly to even think of that question. Turning five brought many new adventures and lots of inquiries.

Back at my home, two houses down and across the street from the Pierces', it was Thanksgiving. Holidays were some of the worst days, especially in our alcoholic home. My father was a mean drunk, who often yelled when he had had too much. He was the reason that kids were not allowed upstairs in our three-story house. It was also why big tables in the house became great places to hide. The house rules were precise and meant to be followed or else! Since the house was usually in total chaos, no one enforced the rules. That day, there was more drinking than usual (as if that was possible) and more stress because everybody was supposed to be happy and grateful. Remember, it was Thanksgiving. Everyone was sitting at the dining room table and the chef, my father, was bringing the turkey from the kitchen. Rarely did these family dinners happen and more rarely did my father cook them. In any case, as he rounded the corner of the kitchen, his shoulder hit the wall phone, which jarred the tray holding the turkey, and the rest took place in slow motion.

First, there was cussing, then yelling, and then I just ran to my room, so I missed what happened next. Yes, it was another happy holiday at the Williams'. The volatility was also the first event that triggered my lifelong coping skill of running away. I took Duke, my only friend, and we retreated to the sand dunes where I had my secret fort.

I hope every kid is lucky enough to have a top-secret hideaway. Tall sea oats, a couple of very scraggly trees, some sand burrs surrounded the fort, and it had a floor of an old cardboard box that Duke and I had dragged there from the Hambroughs' trash can. That way, we didn't get stuck by those awful stickers that were growing everywhere. I was the king of the fort and Duke was the queen. Sometimes we reversed roles.

* * *

The new neighbors were moving in and getting settled. One girl was a grade above me and one girl a class below and then, there was their good-looking brother who was two heads above all of us. All the neighborhood kids went to public school, including the Pierces. My parents insisted that I go to private school, wear a uniform, not ride the school bus, and be miserably different. It had been so long since I had played and had fun that I forgot how much "fun" could be. The Pierces ate pizza for dinner. They played card games together and went to the beach every weekend to swim and play volleyball. Almost every evening right after dinner, Jane, the youngest daughter, pulled out the Ouija board and took it to their front porch. She and her older sister would sit cross-legged on the cold cement, lay their hands on the plastic board, and wait for answers to the future.

If they liked the results, they would yell to their mom, who would be inside cleaning up after dinner, or to their dad, who would be watching TV, that according to the magical answer board, they were getting new bikes, or some other great fate was about to occur. It is a kind of game. Jane told me that if she yelled to her parents what letters were spelled out, it was going to happen. It is too bad that you cannot really pick your parents.

*　*　*

My parents never went to the beach, and at seven I could not understand why. What was even more difficult to comprehend was why didn't Carrie, the maid, or Johnny, her husband, take me to the beach? Maybe it was because Carrie was short and fat and would not look good in a bathing suit. Johnny had a mustache and a scruffy beard, but when he wore shorts, he looked fairly good. All they needed to do was walk over the dunes and watch me swim awhile.

Carrie and Johnny lived in our basement. There were three small bedrooms down there, a bathroom, a small kitchen, and a living room area with a black and white television. The extra bedrooms were where my little brother and sister took their naps. The living room opened up to a substantial paved area where there was room for bikes, the swing set, and the clothesline. Carrie did all the laundry and hanged everything outside to dry. There was no dryer, just the washing machine, which made a lot of noise and irritated the hell out of Johnny. "Turn that damn thing off" was his mantra when he was watching TV, which was most of the day. I did not think he had a job because Johnny did nothing but smoke cigarettes, drink Jim Beam whiskey, and irritate Carrie. I was in the basement too much. We had this huge house, and most of it was off-limits to us kids, even when my parents were not home. I spent a lot of time with Carrie and often wondered, *what is a maid?* She did wear a light-blue dress with a white apron and called it her uniform. She did talk differently, and I had no idea why some of her words all ran together in a sentence and were hard to understand. The washing machine was the "warsher," and "ya'llgitowside" translated for us to get outside. I loved Carrie. She was always helpful to me, even when she was yelling at me or correcting me when I punched my brother in the arm. We laughed a lot, whether it was something funny on the TV or some stupid thing that my siblings, Hunter or Lynn, had done. Carrie tried to protect my younger brother, sister, and me, but she could only do so much.

One day the truth would come out, and all would realize what terrible things took place in that basement. In the meantime, I was still pestering Carrie to take me to the beach. She took my hand and practically dragged me out the door, down the driveway, to where the boardwalk to the beach began. She pointed to a sign that I had never noticed and could not read at the time. Carrie told me that it said, "No Colored on the Beach." Then she said, "We're colored." That was the only answer that I ever got back then. It would be years before Rosa Parks defined what that meant and stood up to the challenge of overcoming racial discrimination. I heard the word "nigger" for the first time that summer after the Pierces moved in, but that was not the last time.

Every Tuesday in the summer, Carrie would babysit her two-year-old granddaughter, Betty. My new best friend, Jane Pierce, and I would take this very precious black baby in my wagon for rides up and down the block. When I say block, I need to explain where I spent my youth. There was the commercial part of the town and the residential part which was divided up into blocks from 31st street all the way to 89th street, and then there was an army base complete with a lighthouse.

We lived on 67th street, Rehoboth Beach, in Virginia. Atlantic Avenue divided the residential section into land side and ocean side and was referred to as the North End. Not only did we live on the ocean side, but we lived on the oceanfront, which meant we were supposed to be rich. After all, we had a maid, both parents worked, we went to private schools, and we were terribly unhappy. I grew up thinking wealth meant misery. As a youngster, it was embarrassing to be the rich kid on the block, and I often pretended that I didn't live in that oceanfront home. However, I loved 67th street, ocean side and land side, and all the people that I knew growing up there, everybody except my family and the nerdy Hambroughs. It would be years and years before I would find out that those folks knew that I had it rough as a kid. Those two matching convertible Bonnevilles in our driveway did nothing to replace the unhappiness and horror that went on inside that three-story house on the dunes.

Back to the story of this little colored baby. Jane and I would stop off at different neighbors to show off our new tiny playmate and would not understand why some people were less than cordial and not receptive to our visits. Perhaps, one was taught racial prejudice, and it would be years before either of us girls would get that horrific lesson.

Still searching, I kept asking myself the question, *Why can't Mr. Pierce be my father?* Well, the best thing to do was to pretend and join their family whenever possible. I used to hide across the street from the Pierces' home behind a trash can holder and wait until they finished their dinner. The garbage cans smelled like vomit, but it was the best place to hide out where I could see the Pierce's dining room. Then, after they ate, I could knock on the door and walk into their family once more. Unfortunately, I had been spending so much time at their home; Mrs. Pierce, whom everyone called Joan, was sending me back to my house when they had their family dinners. Since family time or family dinners did not exist at our house, it was best to hide behind the trash cans and wait patiently for the right time to ring the Pierces' doorbell.

*　*　*

Precocious was another accurate description uttered by my mother to describe me. She could not understand why I challenged her authority and began at an early age to talk back. I did seem to be more curious than most. Since there were rooms in our house where I was not allowed to go, it made them very tempting. The upper floor and attic were pretty much forbidden. *Why should I ever want to go up there?*

Everything I might have needed or wanted was taken care of by Carrie and her husband, Johnny, in the basement. In fact, Johnny was always especially nice to me and brought me candy from the Army base a few blocks away. He also liked to snuggle close, but only when Carrie was not around or not watching. Often, Johnny smelled so bad. He reeked of cigarette smoke and some other unknown odor that resembled dog poop. It was right after lunch, when he patted the sofa next to him. "Come, sit with me and watch some television." Then, he asked me to go into his bedroom and climb into his bed with him. Being very naïve and starving for attention, I enthusiastically followed him into the small, dark bedroom. It only had one window that was odd-shaped. It ran length wise for about four feet and was only one foot high. That is why the light was poor even in the middle of the day. Johnny flicked on a bed lamp and we climbed on top of the covers. I guess that I felt less lonely. I know how scared I felt.

That day I was sexually abused for the first time, and no one knew, or no one chose to do anything about it. That incident was one event that confirmed in my mind that Johnny was acting weird and it would be best to keep those encounters as one of the family secrets. Color had nothing to do with what happened, and for a while, I so wanted him to be my father. He apparently loved me and knew that I needed to be touched and held. It indeed was better than nothing. Deep down, I knew that was bad. At my house, things were bad or good. There was no such thing as sick or well. When I was a middle-aged adult, I learned the difference. But at that time, I was just another nine-year-old girl blaming myself for being molested.

Jane Pierce did become my absolute best friend. We even became blood buddies by sticking our fingers with a needle and pushing our blood drops together, which we had seen performed on TV. The tiny prick seemed disproportionately painful at the time. We only did that ceremony once. Even though she was a year younger, we liked to do all the same things. Jane was willing to share her most important asset, her parents. I continued to live at the Pierces' whenever possible and avoided my alcoholic hellhole that my family called home. Not to mention, Johnny was still there and drunk most of the time. Making sense of the situation was hard. Johnny's wife, Carrie, usually threw him out once a month when he was inebriated. On many occasions, she just turned her back, and he stayed in the basement drinking, waiting for an opportunity to sexually abuse me, my younger sister, or my younger brother.

Johnny used to smoke in bed and still smelled like someone just farted. One day his mattress caught on fire from a burning cigarette. There was smoke, and someone called the fire department. My biggest concern was how to go out to the driveway without being seen coming from Johnny's basement bedroom. Sirens on fire engines still remind me of that awful day. My shirt was off, and I just ran to my special place in the dunes so that no one would see me.

***

It was in the fort that I used to play house and create the family I wanted. By using broken sea oats as little sticks and building a new family home, I pretended there was a happy mommy, a good daddy, and that my older brother would come home from boarding school. He had been sent there two years ago and only came back in the summers. That left me as the oldest, the accountable one. I tried to take care of and be responsible for my younger sister, Lynn, and my younger brother, Hunter. They got all the attention from my parents, and despite the jealousy, I knew that I was in charge of Lynn's and Hunter's safety. I was very envious of how my father doted over my younger brother. One time he came home from work with a miniature car for Hunter. It was bright yellow with a white racing stripe and operated on a battery by pushing the pretend gas throttle. All the kids in the neighborhood gathered around my little brother and his new car for the maiden trip down the driveway and on to the street. I did hate all the attention that Hunter received that day and was especially distraught that I could not take my turn in this new car, as I did not even fit behind the steering wheel. My emotional response was very conflicting. I wanted to see Hunter happy, but I wanted persons to notice me more. That trek through life was very confusing and was on fast forward for the next few years.

There were some notable occurrences during my childhood and some comic relief for the real-life soap opera that kept getting worse. The slobbering dog who followed me everywhere also liked the Pierce home better than his own. Duke was always welcomed in their home and they had a rust-colored Collie, named Venus, who was his girlfriend. There was the holiday incident of the neighborhood that continued as a family saga for many years. One unforgettable, infamous

Thanksgiving, before our family had sat down to eat their big turkey feast, there was a knock at the front door. It seemed that the Pierces were preparing to sit down to their family dinner with relatives from Richmond when Duke jumped up on their kitchen counter, grabbed their twenty-pound turkey, and dragged it into their front yard. After a mad chase down the street, ordinarily patient and kind, an extremely agitated Mr. Pierce knocked on our door and reported the theft. It was too late for their turkey. Fortunately for Duke, he also knew how to hide in the dunes.

My story does have some good memories as my mother tried to hold together her dysfunctional family. Mother was exceptionally beautiful, always concerned about her looks, and extremely outgoing. She had an average height, was medium-built, and had dyed blond hair. She was always on some diet with a weird name, and the diet of the month was the Mayo diet with 500 eggs, or so it seemed. A visit to the hairdresser was scheduled every Tuesday, and nothing was to ever interfere with that appointment with Miss Florette. Mother wore a lot of makeup, especially red lipstick, and always wore shoes that had high heels. I could not balance to walk in them when I sneaked into my mother's clothes closet. Many people told me that I looked like my mother. *Whatever!* I never called her anything but Mother, not Mom or Mommy. It did seem kind of odd, since my friends never called their moms Mother. She talked to everyone she met like she had known them for years but had no close friends. No one ever came to visit my mother, and she spent most of her time at the real estate and construction office. The neighbors said our family was wealthy, and it was because Dottie, my mother, was a brilliant lady and highly active in the man's business world. *What did that mean?*

There were some family vacations and camping trips worth remembering. Mother packed up my younger brother and sister, all the camping gear, and headed for Kerr Dam in central Virginia, also called Buggs Island. It was a beautiful large lake where we kept a boat and had reserved camping sites right on the shoreline. The big house on the oceanfront was left empty, and many people thought it very strange that the Williams would retreat to an inland lake in the summertime when the beach was perfect. Water skiing, hiking, roasting marshmallows, and that is where the good times ended.

My father was to join us on the weekend. He arrived too drunk to drive across the dam to the campsite, so I was put behind the wheel of the station wagon and told to follow my mother, who would be driving the other car. I had never sat behind the wheel of an automobile before. The terror that I felt that day wiped out all the good times of that camping trip. The insanity of having a ten-year-old drive a car was very typical of our household. But what about Janet in all this? *Me?*

It was my first panic attack. The sexual abuse that previous summer rated low on the Richter scale compared to this. My breathing was shallow; my palms were sweaty; my heart was pounding out of my chest; and I was afraid to do or say anything. I could barely see over the steering wheel. I pushed the gas pedal and slowly followed my mother's car. I imagined myself on a tight wire, and I knew if I turned the steering wheel a half inch either way, I would go right off the bridge. I made it and came down with an excruciating earache the remainder of the camping trip. I could not wait to get home to the beach.

***

No one knew that the following Friday was going to be a day that changed my life forever. We all have those days, some good, some bad. I was so innocent and had totally lost my childhood. It was no wonder that I wanted to rebel, break the rules, and be weird with my friends, to get attention and acceptance.

It was a typical Friday when my mother and father went off to work. Johnny was missing for a couple of weeks, and Carrie was downstairs, cleaning. That was the other thing about our house. It had to be perfect. In fact, just last weekend, a photographer had come to take pictures of the interior of our house, including my room, for an advertisement that my parents were running to bring more business to their construction firm. My job was to put on a dress with a pinafore and pose in my bedroom as a happy child. Since I never, ever wore dresses, it was a performance and not a pleasant one. So, looking and acting the part became another character trait I adopted. It would prove to cause significant problems in my future.

Being perfect sets an extremely high standard. Some of you can probably relate with that feeling. Always falling short of expectations and still planning the outcomes leads to constant disappointment and self-loathing. I am now seeking approval from everyone that I meet. I was learning incredibly early in life that if I brought home straight As on my report card, I got my father's attention. He signed my report card and seemed to be enormously proud of me. That 4.0 average was a standard of excellence that followed me into college.

Let's go back to the infamous Friday at the Williams' house. The baggage trunk was brown with reinforced metal on the corners and had a metal hinge but no lock. You only needed to push a button to open the chest. Jane and I were up in the dark attic, a forbidden room. There was an overhead light with a string hanging down. I was standing on a box and yank on the line. No, we did not have permission. But with everyone gone or busy, it was the perfect time to go poking around where we were not supposed to. I did not know what we expect, but a rabbit did not jump out, and there were no mouse traps. On the contrary, we only found lots and lots of papers and several photo albums. One photo was of a man in a military uniform, and there were several pictures of my older brother when he was young, standing next to this man. Bruce King was the name on the photo. Jane was looking through some of the papers and said to me, "Whoa!" She got my attention. We both tried to make sense out of the documents which appeared to be adoption papers with my name on them. And more importantly, they had my birthday listed as the day after I had been celebrating my birthday for all the previous years. That must have been a big mistake, because my birthday was November 24, not November 25. Not fully understanding what I was seeing, I slammed the trunk lid shut, ordered Jane out of the attic, told my best friend to go home, and tried to figure out what to do.

* * *

Sometimes the wind blew just enough to help the sea oats dance. They would sway back and forth and seem to have their own individual beat. There was something extraordinary about drawing in the sand, making little sandcastles and small houses and tearing them down and building new ones. Sitting in my secret spot under the old cypress trees was not only a great hiding place, but it was also a place of refuge. I would go there to get away, but waiting to be found was my chief motive. No one ever came looking.

Instead of running to the dunes after the attic discovery, I was waiting in the upstairs hallway for my mother to come home from work. I kept staring at the photo, on the wall, of my cute little brother and sister on some playground, laughing and having fun. The more I studied that photo, the angrier I got. *Why are they so happy and I am so miserable?* I followed her into her clothes closet and did not even pause until she had changed from her work clothes before I blurted out the question: "Why didn't you tell me I was adopted? Why have you been celebrating my birthday on a wrong day?" My mother's "What are you talking about?" was not the answer I wanted to hear, and it did not go down very well. I was distraught and did not care about getting in trouble about being in the attic. I just wanted answers before my fake father, or whoever he was, came home. My mother did not mince words and told me that it was true, meaning that it was one big lie. I was adopted when I was five. In a business-like tone, my mother told me that my real father died in a plane crash when I was two. He was the man in the military uniform, named Bruce King. And, by the way, she told me, she did not know why I was upset, as she was my real mother. I listened, sort of, and wondered about that word, "real." *What is a "real" mother?* She offered no explanation, and I sat there crying and confused. About my birthday, she said she had just made a little mistake. *A little mistake?* I could not believe that she thought that was a little mistake. But more important! Now, I knew who my father was not. I knew for sure that it was not this man who had been calling himself my father. It was not this violent, drunk man who did not love me. My father was the man in that picture. He was all dressed up in some kind of military uniform and looked kind of scary. But he was also good-looking. *Why did my mother lie to me?* The answer is extremely complicated and would not be understood for many, many years.

After the face-off with my mother, I headed for my fort. No one, not even Jane, knew about my hideaway. It did not matter how cold or dark it was, that's where I went. Usually, Duke was by my side. At times, it could be terrifying, but this time, I was sure that someone would come find me and bring me home. I had cried after all. No one showed up. Again. I sat for a long time, more minutes than an hour. I know because I was counting. No one came to find me.

I had questions that needed answers. Essential situations, like Father's Day posed new problems for me. *Should I still give this father a Father's Day card when he was not even my father? Why didn't he tell me the truth? Did he never go to the beach because he did not like me? Or was he embarrassed to be around me because I was not his real daughter?* While I hid, I wove the sea oats together in a braid and then let the sand run through my hands. I could see the seagulls glide over the tops of the dunes, and it looked like they never had to use their wings. They made it look so fun. It really was the first time that I really looked at a bird. They seemed to have it so easy just soaring over the dunes, going up and down with the air currents, always watching to see what was below. And by choice, the seagulls would often land on the sand and beg beachcombers for treats. They could not run fast on the beach and would suddenly take off and cruise over the ocean. *What a great thing to be able to do!* The gulls distracted me for a few minutes, but I was still despondent. My mother told me that "big girls don't cry."

I did begin to cry and felt very guilty when the tears came cascading down my cheeks. In fact, that day the floodgates opened, and I sobbed. I was not entirely sure why. Duke rolled over on his side and provided much-needed warmth and comfort to the sad little girl under the trees.

After confronting my mother and having so many questions go unanswered, I needed to run away, far away. It would take me a long time to sort out the other relationships, like who was my biological brother, who are halves?

Fourth grade was significant. How do you go to school and admit to your friends, to your classmates, that your mother messed up your birth date? I had to do it. I started on the playground and just let a few kids know at a time to see what their reaction would be. They laughed. My best friend, Jane, went to a different school, so she was already spreading the rumors there. "Did you know that Janet is adopted and her birthday is on the wrong day?" It turned out not to be a massive deal in elementary school, but many, many years later it still bothered me a lot.

* * *

I continued to spend every waking moment I could at the Pierces', and if I was not in their home, I was across the street in the shrubs, looking in, and wishing I were in their family room. During those lonely times, I spent a great deal of time with Duke, running away. I did not go far because it was too cold or I was too afraid. It would not be long before family roles in the Williams' house would change, but right now I was the scapegoat and took a lot of scolding and punishments that should not have come my way. I could not even tell Jane about these. After all, I had to protect those family secrets and make sure everyone thought that we had the perfect loving family. And then, there were the "things" with Johnny. That is what I called them. They were getting worse. He didn't even care if his wife, Carrie, was around or not.

* * *

It was an unusually sunny day and not too hot. Since it was Saturday, we were off from school, but no one was on the beach in late October. Looking back on the entire episode, I do not think I meant to cause anyone any harm. It really was child's play. It had only been two weeks since the accident. Our neighbor, Mr. Hambrough, the father of the nerdy girls, had died. Jane and I were on the Hambroughs' front lawn reenacting his demise. Unfortunately, Mrs. Hambrough was the audience, and her husband's death was a suicide by hanging (knocking a chair out from under himself). We acted out all the ugly details. It was quite a performance. Mrs. Hambrough went screaming into her home. I learned that people do feel and react, especially at a time of crisis like the death of a loved one. It was a life lesson that I would not forget.

Coincidentally, on the home front, my older half-brother, Edward, aged sixteen, had been hospitalized for something. I was told that it was not serious because he was just trying to get attention from our stepfather. The family went to Richmond to visit him in the psychiatric hospital, and that was a new experience. There were locked doors at the entrance, and you had to ring a bell to get someone to open the door. You had to leave car keys, pens, or any sharp objects in a plastic bin. *Why would they ask my parents to do that?* Identification was required, and the nurse reminded the family that visiting time was limited to half hour and children—myself, and my younger brother and sister— were not allowed. No one talked about the visit to see Edward, or how he was getting along. Apparently, he was also asking, "Are you really my father?" and dealing with his new road to life, which included a stepfather that did not like or love him. Feelings were mutual, and physically they were at different poles. Our stepfather was six feet, four inches and 240 pounds, had graying hair, and rarely smiled. Edward was five feet, nine inches, if he stood on his tiptoes, weighed 125 pounds, and usually had a plastic smirk on his face.

I was never very close to Edward, and it could be the eight-year age difference. No, there was something else there. It would be a long time before I understood what Edward was going through and just how alone he felt at that time. No one ever called him Ed or Eddie, like at my school. In my family, we just seemed more formal, and using full names was the right thing to do. I never heard the word Dad or Daddy. In any case, Edward was my only biological brother, according to the adoption papers in the attic. That was also a lie and would not be uncovered for many, many years.

* * *

Activities in the neighborhood included butt-busting and boogie-boarding on the beach, volleyball, roller-skating, and doing what "normal" kids do. I guess. Kick the can was one game that happened on the street almost every evening. One person was "it," and everyone else was supposed to go hide in the scratchy bushes, behind neighboring houses, or in the dunes, my dunes. If you ran to home base and successfully kicked the old coffee can before being tagged, you were safe. My strategy was to wait until all my friends had been caught or were safely at "home" and then sneak in amidst the chaos.

It is interesting as that is precisely what I was doing in my dysfunctional home. If I stayed quiet and out of sight, I avoided the constant drama.

About this time a bit of a miracle occurred. A trampoline appeared in my backyard. It was a special gift from my parents and became the favorite spot where my friends and I spent most of our time when we weren't on the beach. There were trampoline shows for the parents, neighbors, and visiting tourists. My friends and I became amazingly professional in our flips, flops, twists, and turns. Having the trampoline made me popular. No one was allowed in the house, but the play yard brought my friends over to my property, and that was wonderful. It created a whole new activity, and we were outstanding.

Who could have guessed that I would continue flipping and bouncing into my teens? In high school, I would have the privilege of learning and teaching trampoline with the famous "Flying Wallendas." In fact, my high school in Florida was the home of "The Sailor Circus" which was sponsored by Ringling Brothers, Barnum, and Bailey. Students from my school performed in the circus. Little did I know that my "jumping" days in childhood would prepare me for such a fantastic and fun sport in the future.

Stop! I am getting ahead of myself. Back to the elementary school years. Older brother, Edward, was home in the summer of 1960. He brought home a pole vault which he was using to compete in sports trials at his boarding school. I could not wait to try it and vaulted right over the front lawn shrubbery onto a huge log that was lying loosely on the ground. I did not see the sizable piling until I landed on it and broke my leg. This was very typical of "leaping before you look." My compulsivity was becoming more and more apparent. So much for pole vaulting!

To this day, I have no idea why, for that particular school year, I was sent to public school (with the Pierce kids) for fifth grade. Perhaps my whining and complaining finally made a difference. It was my dream come true. Arriving on crutches made me an instant center of attention. My new classmates took turns having races on my crutches down the hallway. My crutches! If you remember fifth grade, all of this was a big deal. I wanted to be liked by everyone. It was imperative to be chosen on the right team in physical education and not be the last to be selected, or not picked at all. Of course, this was in between the atomic bomb drills during the Cuban missile crisis in 1961. The same year Alan Shepard circumnavigated the earth in a space capsule. His daughter happened to be in my classroom. When my mother dropped me off at school, she brought our TV and carried it inside to lend to my teacher, Mrs. Washburn. The entire class watched my television to see Commander Shepard up in space. My TV! For the first time, in an awfully long time, I felt special, like a celebrity, and even made some friends. No one teased me about being adopted. This hiatus from the hard journey of life was very short-lived, but I made the most of it.

* * *

The following summer, my stepfather was diagnosed with cancer, a brain tumor, and was given less than a year to live. By this time, I was exceptionally good at putting on different hats and performing different roles. I was becoming entirely independent of my family and beginning to look outside my home for comfort, for support, and for love.

Falling out of the nest so young meant that the mother bird did not teach me how to fly and I had to learn on my own. This flight included finding a way to forgive my mother and knowing more about my deceased father in the military hat.

At this time sperm banks were making the news, along with artificial insemination and freezing embryos. I was not aware of all the hoopla, but many women and men saw these new methods as an opportunity to parent, and I heard kids talk about it at school. It seemed to be "cool" at the time, so I told several teachers and classmates that I was adopted. I even pretended that my mother was not my biological parent, but that she had also adopted me. It made me feel twice as "cool." However, on the inside, I was beginning to feel terribly angry, fearful, and resentful that I had never met my real father in the old photo. I wanted to ask him what the military uniform was about. *Did he run the country and shoot bad guys? Was he ever in a war?* Since he had died when I was two, I could not remember ever meeting or seeing him. I just knew that he would have been better than what I got. He had a big smile on his face in the photo, was especially important looking in his naval uniform, and was attractive too. One big problem—he was dead and gone.

September brought new changes that could not be explained and were equally difficult to accept. I was transferred to the local parochial school for sixth grade. I was only in public school for one year. I loved it and could not believe that I was being torn away from my new school to attend another one. In fact, the whole family was converted to Catholicism, and that meant lots of change. It was my stepfather's idea, and I hated him for taking me away from my friends in public school. Once again, I was the odd man out, felt isolated, and missed riding the bus with the Pierce kids.

It was about this time that my mother drove Hunter and Lynn to Florida for an unexpected visit to our grandmother's. My Grandma Lee and my step-grandfather, Lynn, lived just outside of Tampa, Florida. I was left home alone with my stepfather. It could have been a disaster if it were not for the vast Ash Wednesday flood of 1962. Living in a home that was right on the oceanfront meant facing many hurricanes over the years. I remember these construction workers putting up big plywood boards to cover our enormous plate glass windows in the living room and upstairs in my parents' bedroom. It made the house dark but supposedly safe from the winds and flying debris. However, we had not seen any hurricane like this advancing maelstrom. It was the perfect storm. There really were not big gusts of wind, but there were big surges of water. The ocean came over the dunes, and the bay flooded the inland waterways to completely engulf the town. The streets were covered with flood waters, and it kept rising. Houses were deluged, and mass evacuations were ordered. Oblivious to this turn of events, my stepfather decided that he would get me to school in his Bonneville convertible. My mother and younger brother and sister were still down south in Florida. So, my stepfather ordered me to the car, and we set out for my school. Even as the water began seeping under the car doors, he was reluctant to turn back. Being self-centered in the extreme, he did not care about evacuations. He was going to rise above the storm and do what he wanted to do. It was leaking through the windows, and we finally turned around to go back home, just in the nick of time.

We hear every so often that good times, and great things can come out of adversity. It is true! My house was on a hill and the only home on the block that did not flood. Contrary to my stepfather's typical reaction, he walked down the street and invited those afflicted by the flood to move into our house until the water subsided. The Pierces came to our house to live temporarily and wait out the tide. It was fantastic! My favorite family was living in my house. It was like a real home for the next six days. There were no alcoholic outbursts, and even the maid and her husband, Johnny, behaved. I had never had such a great pajama party and never wanted it to end.

Unfortunately, the flood waters did subside. The Pierces moved back to their home, which had eight inches of mud throughout every room, and mother returned from Florida. Everyone could resume their unhappy, unhealthy family roles.

***

There were so many house rules, "dos" and "don'ts," and little communication. I was not allowed to have my best friend, Jane, to spend the night. Every time my mother came home from work, she immediately sent Jane to her home. Jane did not understand, and neither did I. Years later, Jane finally asked: "Why couldn't I ever spend the night at your house? Why was your mother so mean to me?" I did my best to describe alcoholism to her and all the secrets and odd behaviors that were part of my growing up. Twelve-year-olds do a poor job of explaining all this. Just like adults!

It is said that the only thing constant in life is change. This was definitely true in the Williams family. My mother decided a geographical cure would fix everything and moved away from the beach, apart from the Pierces, and away from my secret place in the dunes. Moving to another neighborhood did not fix my mother's unhappy marriage, pull our family closer together, or hide all our imperfections. Jane would be the last close female friend that I would ever have, and I had not even reached adolescence.

One of the fallouts of catching my mother in so many lies is that I did not have any trust left. I had trusted Carrie, Johnny, my older brother, and look where that got me. It was inconceivable that a family could have lived so many lies, and I was only twelve years old.

The move to a new neighborhood fixed some things. The sexual abuse stopped. Carrie was fired. The Pierces were now on the other side of town near the beach, and we moved to a small rental house fifteen miles away. We were not living in the biggest house, and the new one was ugly. It was a ranch house with white bricks and a ridiculously small yard. My mother tried to sell us all the benefits like a real estate agent. She said, "All of these changes are for you. We are moving so everything can be worked out. This change is for all of us to start over." I did not know what she meant and was not asking for any explanations. I did know that moving from an awfully expensive, contemporary home on the oceanfront did not compare with this small rental home in the middle of some subdivision, somewhere.

* * *

Doctors came and went out of the new house. Business associates met, discussed, and made decisions. And there were the hospitals. My stepfather had two major operations, chemotherapy, seizures, and physical therapy. It all happened, and most of the time, I felt like a spectator looking in. I hovered like a seagull watching from above and witnessed all the chaos. I do remember those moments vividly, and if I shut my eyes, the events unfold over and over again.

One very rainy afternoon in that rental house, which we were supposed to call home, I purposefully hid in the bathroom not far from my stepfather's bed. I tried to eavesdrop on what his friend, Dr. Hartman, was telling him, and I heard, "It won't be long now, Al." I forgot his name was Al. In fact, rarely did my mother call him anything. I did not call him Dad since I found out he was my stepfather. Maybe I should have called him Al. Whatever! The doctor just told him that he did not have to wait much longer. *What did that mean?* I found out three years later, on the anniversary of his death. My stepfather went in and out of hospice four times. Finally, his doctor friend gave him enough morphine to put him to sleep permanently. Now-a-days they call it a "mercy-killing" or "suicide assistance." At the time it did not seem right. No one criticized the decision or objected to its execution.

* * *

After our family converted to Catholicism, there were some major changes which continued after our move away from the beach house. There were no choices, no options, when it came to my future. I was forced into the parochial school, left my friends at public school, and embraced all the new changes as best as I could.

My two years at the local parochial school were a total immersion into Catholicism, and I learned that some people do have strict routines and often, there was no flexibility. Every morning my classmates met in the chapel to participate in morning prayers before class began. Every Wednesday there was a full mass before going to our classroom. Saturday mornings were reserved for catechism, sort of the Catholic Sunday School. Part of me embraced these expectations because there were not any routines in our chaotic family. There was no school bus, which meant one of my parents would have to drive me to and from school. My stepfather usually took the morning shuttle, and my mother would pick me up at the end of the day. The rides to school were typically quiet, and my mother was episodically late for pickups. I continued to do well scholastically and did enjoy all the fanfare of First Communion, May Day, and the other religious holidays.

***

"Hold on to your bootstraps, Janet, things are really going to hit the fan."

"It is best for you if you get out of the family for awhile, Janet, and I cannot really handle you the way things are." My mother was preparing me for the near future, and I did not see it. She was talking about sending me away, far away. "What did I do to deserve this? Being a tween is not always easy, but am I that bad?"

Fast forward to eighth grade and the Catholic boarding school where I would live for the next year. It is located in the foothills of the Blue Ridge Mountains, near Asheville, North Carolina, about an eight-hour drive from our home.

I hated it. Being the perfectionist that life demanded, I received two distinguished awards from that school that indeed indicated an internal conflict. I was given a trophy for the highest grade average in religious studies and a certificate for getting the most demerits any student had ever acquired. The habit of running away was present in boarding school, and quite compulsively, I would leave the school grounds and walk to the nearest town of Asheville. It was unquestionably an excellent way to accumulate demerits and be grounded in detention during any free or play times.

It was during the fall term when the leaves were on the ground, and there was a cold front that moved us indoors. With a group of girls, I was watching the infamous parade on television when John F. Kennedy was shot and killed in broad daylight. The entire tragedy was broadcast live, and everyone sat in horror as the future of the country changed forever. My classmates were crying, and I felt like crying. Almost everyone remembers where they were the moment that assassination took place. It was three days before my birthday, and I still feel guilty for thinking that the timing was bad, as it would make people sad on my birthday. Being entirely self-centered, like most young teens, the question was how could it happen on that particular weekend? No one would want to sing a birthday song, and the total focus would be on the President of the United States and not me. However, it was Christmas of that year that propelled me into a new road to life.

* * *

The table was set for seven. There were cloth napkins on the table and seven cereal bowls. I sat down and began to pour my muesli wondering if I should wait for everyone else to sit down. Edward started eating. This was supposed to be my stepfather's last Christmas (dying from cancer), which was why everyone was at the table.

I was sent an airline ticket at my boarding school in North Carolina, and Mother Superior took me to the airport. Her words of wisdom were to pray, and everything would work out as God was the director. I had no idea what she was talking about. I flew down to Key West by myself to meet the rest of the family. It was my first flight, and it was terrifying. Children traveling alone on airplanes are treated very nicely, which made the trip seem a little like an adventure. I got to meet the pilot, got a unique airline pin, and sat right up front near the cabin. I just did not realize what the destination would look like. My boarding school experience for the past five months had been stormy, to say the least. The trip would be a piece of cake and definitely a vacation for me, or so I thought. I needed a break from the controlling nuns, and they certainly needed a break from me. As I was on my flight, I remembered my last caper at boarding school. I had always wondered if the nuns shaved their heads. It had been rumored that there was not one hair on the sisters' heads. On a routine Friday night my roommate and I noticed a large cardboard box in the hallway right down from Sister Monica's bedroom. We decided to cut peepholes in the cardboard, hide in the box for the night, and witness firsthand the nun going to the bathroom without her habit. Two surprises! Sister Monica had a head full of hair, and she knew we were there the entire evening. More demerits.

* * *

Back to the "last" Christmas. My mother had called this family gathering to stay at a rented house on the water somewhere in the Florida Keys. It had a dock, a boat, and a gorgeous view of the open sea. You could see fishing trawlers on the horizon and large yachts with extended outriggers and hanging nets. The holiday visit included the guest of honor, my stepfather, his first wife, Mrs. Williams #1, and a daughter, Cynthia, by his first marriage. She was the same age as me. All our immediate family was in attendance. Two Mrs. Williams? This certainly made for an exciting breakfast.

Mrs. Williams #1 sat down and placed a handgun, a real loaded gun, above her coffee cup. Nobody said anything. The revolver looked like something on the TV show *Lone Ranger*. I found out later that she just liked to have it at all meals and she took it back to her bedroom during the day and night. *Was she going to kill us or was she that paranoid?* I did find out after that pilgrimage that she had some "issues" that caused her behavior. And who doesn't?

My stepfather's other daughter, older than me by two weeks, is everything that I am not. Cynthia is two feet taller (slight exaggeration), has perfect skin, perfect teeth, and is very artistic with her watercolors and oil paints. She has not a humorous bone in her body and enjoys anything inactive, like reading or sleeping. Mrs. Williams #1 had obviously had a role with this teen who needed severe revision. I could not stand her even before she said "hello." I had to find a way to avoid her for the next four weeks that everyone spent together waiting for the stepfather to die.

Finding an escape from that crazy family reunion was difficult. My older brother came to the rescue. He liked to take the boat out and go fishing. I tagged along and not only learned about boats and fishing but also bonded with my older brother in a unique way that was not conditional on anything or anyone.

* * *

It was not the last Christmas "goodbye" that it was supposed to be because my stepfather lived another eighteen months. After returning to boarding school, things went from bad to worse for me. I had discovered boys but was too fat and too ugly to do anything about it. Besides, it was an all-girls school. I waited for the telephone call from my mother that my stepfather had died. There were very few phone calls from home, and most were to remind me that the school was costly, so I had better do better and shape up. I was shaping up by getting fatter and fatter, bordering on obesity. Eating was a way to get comfort, feel good, and be sociable. There was no beach, no sand dunes and it was not a place where you learned to spread your wings and fly. The weight gain was judged as disgusting by my mother who was totally immersed in her husband's illness. Being fat and being obsessed with body image would be an issue for the rest of my journey through life.

* * *

Al's cancer ate away slowly at his brain, and some major decisions were made which affected everybody in the family. He requested to die at home, so our house became a morgue. There was no TV, no radio, and no family. I came home from a Catholic boarding school, and the doctors continued to come and go, stay, and leave.

* * *

I might have forgotten to tell you about my first Sunday School before Catholicism. That being a critical point in my life, I want you to see the course that my spiritual road followed. Before my forced conversion to be Catholic, I would go with the Pierces every Sunday and attend their Presbyterian Church. It was another outing that I looked forward to because I could get dressed up and be with my favorite family, my only functional family. I did own a few frilly dresses, and fancy pointed shiny black shoes that were uncomfortable to wear. I would have preferred jeans and a T-shirt, but no one was asking me. It did not matter, and every Sunday I anticipated a car horn blowing for me to join the back seat of my best friend's station wagon. I really did not know how to pray and would just pretend that pointing my fingers up to the church ceiling meant something.

However, with the onset of cancer, it was my stepfather who had a spiritual awakening. Everything changed. Now we were expected to go to church every Sunday, as a family. I was given no choice in the matter. I did make friends with a few of the nuns that first year, which was opposite to what my future boarding school experience would be. In fact, in sixth grade, I decided it would be cool to become a nun, somebody's sister. This fantasy lasted that entire year. The family was totally engulfed in the Catholic rituals, rules, and routines. I already mentioned my First Communion, and it did get lots of attention. My parents took us all out to lunch at the local diner after the ceremony. We sat up on stools, and I remember spinning my stool and laughing. I do not know what was funny, but everyone was laughing. I wish that day could have gone on forever.

During my three years in a parochial school, I continued to excel academically, but I know why. It was expected, and I still had that unrealistic goal to be perfect. Getting good grades was one way to continue to get approval, to get attention, and to manipulate the rules. In fact, I never got less than an "A" until graduate school. My college "B" occurred when I was hospitalized, and I sent my daughter to tape the classes that I could not attend. My default mode was "it's always someone else's fault."

My spiritual journey continued through Catholic school, and I seriously considered wearing the "habit" as a great way to hide from life. I even went with the nuns to a retreat in Richmond. Tables exhibited all the different religious orders you could join, and some were even cloistered. What a great word and a fascinating concept! This idea would pass.

* * *

How a family handles death is quite impressive. It seems the more dysfunctional a family is with living issues, the more dysfunctional that family will be with dying issues, such as last rites, funerals, grief, monetary estates, and secrets. My stepfather was murdered or was the beneficiary of mercy killing.

Bedridden after his second brain tumor surgery, he begged my mother to put him out of his misery. She could not or would not do it. He slipped in and out of coma for several days, and finally the doctor, who happened to be a friend of the family, gave him a fatal shot of morphine. It was finally over. I was shipped off to the beach for the day. My mother asked a friend to drive me to the beach where I grew up and just leave me there until she could pick me up. The Pierces were out of town, and it was very lonely. My best buddy, Duke, had died, so I walked the beach and sat alone in the dunes most of the afternoon. The July sun was unusually warm that day, and there was nothing to drink. This was poor planning by my mother or whoever was in charge. Before the final morphine shot, everyone was given a turn to say goodbye and told to give him a kiss. I felt like I was kissing a total stranger, but I wanted to be there when he died. After all, he was the only father that I had ever known. He was not my "real" father, and maybe that is why mother did not want me around. In any case, as I was walking along the surf, I actually looked at the ocean and asked God to make things better. I had no idea who God was, but I needed help, and I wanted to believe in someone. In fact, it was that day that the family roles changed forever.

*　*　*

Hunter and Lynn have hardly been mentioned, but they were my younger brother and sister. Correction! My half brother and half sister. Since they were raised and cared for by the housekeeper, Carrie, and quite a bit younger than me, those two were not really a part of my life until the sexual abuse started. I began finding ways to make sure they were never alone with Johnny. To this day I feel incredibly guilty for not telling someone what was going on in the basement. Carrie knew, and she tried to shield the children and protect them, but Johnny's alcoholism got the best of her too. When we moved away from the beach, Johnny and Carrie did not move with us, and that was a good thing and a bad thing. Carrie was the only "mother," except for Mrs. Pierce, that I had ever had. I missed her. She was loving, caring, and did the best she could with two raving alcoholics in the same house, the madam of the house in complete denial, and the kids trying to raise themselves. One time, when I did try to tell my mother what was going on, she laughed and told me I always did have a good imagination. "Go make your bed!"

What were the consequences of this abuse on my younger sister and brother? There are many books on this subject, but their futures were undoubtedly affected. Lynn would never be able to trust or associate with any person of color. All the counseling, hypnosis, and psychiatric treatment did not change this reaction or help her to face the fears of her childhood.

Hunter was an entirely different story. By age eighteen, he was hooked up with Scientology. Kidnapping him and doing systematic deprogramming did not pull him away from his new life, which was founded by Ron Hubbard. Financial ruin, a failed marriage, and the inability to stay in college were part of his adolescence and young adult history. Hunter left our family and never looked back. He had little or no relationship with our mother and had little interaction with his father. Can childhood abuse cause these reactions? Absolutely. I witnessed it firsthand.

* * *

Let's go back to my adolescence. When I enquired about my stepfather's funeral, there were no tears, nor a sad face. I had discovered, on my own, that my stepfather was not a liar, nor a bad person. He was an extremely sick man, psychologically, emotionally, and physically. Years later, I would learn that alcoholism is a disease of the brain which has no cure and affects the entire family. Overnight, after he died, I became the *de facto* parent in the family and was given the responsibility at age thirteen of keeping Hunter and Lynn safe, happy, and out of trouble. It was a tall order. How do you learn to fly in one night?

I had never seen a dead person before. There were lots of people at the funeral, and most of them were complete strangers, except for the Pierces without their kids. I knew a couple of my stepfather's business associates. He looked like a wax figure in a museum, except he was lying down and was cold as an ice cube. How do I know? I touched his forehead. Not many people knew that he had on a wig, but I kept that information to myself. I was worried that someone might lift it and mess it up. My job, as always, was to take care of Hunter and Lynn. "Don't let them go to the funeral!" was my plea to my mother. They were only eight and six years old, respectively, and asked too many questions that I could not answer. Hunter wanted to touch his father, and Lynn was afraid to go anywhere near the casket. Lynn was crying, afraid to even look at what was going to happen next. That made it very tricky. I had to stretch my hands in opposite directions, so everyone stayed happy. It was a funeral, and yet, the family rule was to remain happy.

* * *

Significant change marked the next five years. I lived in five different houses in Virginia, Florida, and finally Switzerland. My mother was trying the geographical cure, looking for men and love in all the new or all the wrong places. Since she always took "her" with her, there were no new long-term personal commitments for my mother or the family. Actually, things got worse for me. As they say, it is not the destination but the journey along the way that deserves attention.

We stayed in that depressing rental home for two years. Not only was it not on the beach, but it sat on a wooded lot with so many trees that the sun never reached the house or the yard. It had dead vines growing on several sides of the house, and it was the place where he died. No sunlight outside and lots of unpacked boxes inside. Fortunately, my mother was building a new home on the river and we just had to wait for completion. By ninth grade we had moved into the new house and were working on a new start for our family.

Being the primary caretaker was a massive order for any teenager and particularly difficult for an angry, disturbed, resentful thirteen-year-old. After my stepfather died, a pattern began to emerge that would follow me into adulthood. I was either very, very good or very, very bad. Perhaps it was that early driving experience over that high dam, but one of my antics was to borrow (steal) one of the family cars when my mother was out and take my friends for joy rides back on old farm roads. Speed was always the goal. The risky behavior that would follow me into adulthood had begun. I would put the pedal to the metal until someone yelled stop. There was never an accident, and I was never caught. Still, no one came to look for me.

The newly built house that we lived in Virginia was very remote, with our closest neighbors being about two city blocks away. However, I did make friends. My best friend was my first young boyfriend, Timmy, and we did everything together. He was a celebrity. His dad was the first POW (prisoner of war) during the Vietnam War and was in the news quite a bit. Timmy really did not like to talk about it, except to me, and most of our time was spent on the river, either sailing, fishing, or crabbing. Looking back there were no sexual feelings in the relationship. We were simply great friends and cohorts in seeking fun and finding trouble. I do not know where I learned about sex, and I do not remember any serious mother–daughter talks. I was very naïve and a late bloomer, but I was starting to look at the opposite sex in an engaging, inquisitive way. Let me describe Timmy to you. He was a "hunk." He was smart, extremely popular, athletic, creative, and extremely sensitive. That would be a prerequisite, as he set the standard for future boyfriends.

* * *

A young couple down the street had a standing date on Friday night, and I got my first job. I was hired as the babysitter for their two-year-old and their six-month-old baby. I really loved babies, but both kids were usually sleeping when I arrived and stayed asleep for the duration of my visit. After two or three sessions, I innocently discovered a bottle of rum in their kitchen. That was a very pivotal moment in my life. I decided to help myself to a shot, or two, while I was babysitting. One night the couple questioned me about the alcohol, and a lie that would last twenty-two years came out of my mouth. "No, I did not touch it." That was my first but, indeed, not my last bad encounter with alcohol. I never babysat for that family again. My mother overlooked the indiscretion and did nothing to punish me and said nothing of the entire episode.

It was a very odd year. One project that caused a few raised eyebrows was the "worm" project. Reading in some magazine, I ran across an advertisement that suggested you could make a great deal of money by investing in bloodworms (yes, you read that right). Investing meant multiplying a dozen worms very quickly and selling them locally to the fishermen at a profit. After building a 4' × 6' wooden box covered with a window screen, I coerced my little brother to help me put it in the front woods by our house. By feeding table scraps to the worms and checking the squiggly things every day, I was successful in breeding lots and lots of bloodworms. Who could have predicted a crisis with a budding cottage industry like growing worms? Someway, somehow, the cover screen was taken off, blown off, or a more massive creature nudged it off, and every bloodworm flew the coup. They were all gone. I was furious and secretly blamed my younger brother, Hunter, for this act of vengeance. It was a great idea, and the goal went up in smoke instead of dollars.

Another ritual which had begun to flourish in my house put even more responsibility on my back. My mother started dating. She was still a beautiful woman, had bleached blond hair, wore the best outfits, and had money. She was obsessed with her figure and continued to weigh all of us on a regular basis. There was no extra fat, even on the dog, the new German Shepherd, Stormy.

I gave my mother specific curfew times, but they were ignored or overlooked. Many a night, you could find me pacing by the front door at one in the morning, angry and resentful. I was worried and fearful for my mother's safety. She was the only parent that I had left. It was years before I realized that there was a major role reversal going on in our house. No wonder that I felt like a young adult rather than a typical thirteen-year-old. It was understood by my younger brother and sister that I was the responsible one; my older brother, Edward, was the crazy one; and our mother was usually missing.

One evening, just after dark, there was some banging on the front door. I went to check it out and saw this guy dripping wet in a drenched suit with his tie half pulled out. He told me to open the door, and I told him Mother was not home. Thinking that would take care of it, I went back to watch television with my younger brother and sister. Two minutes later, the same guy was pounding on the side door near the family room and demanding to be let into the house. Stormy, who was at my side, was barking at the door, but that caused no reaction by the perpetrator. I told him that I was going to call the police if he did not go away. I had seen that work on TV shows, so why not? My voice was a little shaky, and I was terrified. Hunter and Lynn were sent to their room, and I tried to stay in control. I had never called the police, but that man was threatening and would not go away. I ran to the kitchen phone and immediately dialed my friend Timmy. *Why didn't I call the police?* In hindsight, that would have been the smart thing to do. Timmy's mom got on the phone and told me to go join Hunter and Lynn in their bedroom, lock the door, and she was going to call the police. By this time, it was thundering, and the door banging had stopped. We never heard a siren, but in about half an hour, the front doorbell rang. The three of us huddled together in our nighties, made our way to the entryway, and saw that it was a uniformed police officer. Looking back, I went from scared to annoyed very quickly. The policeman had tons of questions that I could not answer, and he acted like I had done something wrong. I felt judged and not taken seriously. "Where is your mother?" That was the first question, and I did not know the answer. The whole experience felt entirely out of my control. It was almost like a bad play that never really happened. No, it was real, but one more thing that no one in our family ever talked about or acknowledged.

My mother's dating did have some benefits. There was the fellow who only wore red socks. It turned out that he was a pilot and believed that his red socks were a good luck charm that would keep him from crashing. He offered my mother free flying lessons. When she declined, they were provided to me. At age fourteen, I was up in the skies flying a little Cessna after school. Unfortunately, that relationship only lasted three months. I fell short of getting my pilot's license, but I did get my driver's license the same year.

That brings our journey to a fellow traveler that was the love of my life, my grandma Lee. She also had a very dysfunctional, shaky childhood. She survived and thrived. I not only shared her middle name but I also adored my grandmother. Grandma was the only one who gave me hugs and told me how much she loved me. It was my grandma that taught me how to play board games and card games. Cribbage was our favorite. It was a time to laugh and enjoy life.

One very memorable occasion was when I was fourteen and Grandma Lee took me in her small Renault to take my driver's license test. Behind the wheel, I was a nervous wreck and had difficulty with the parallel parking that was required. No problem! Grandma Lee distracted the policeman who was assessing my parking performance by talking his ear off. He did not notice the three times that I hit the curve. It was an exceptional day, using my grandmother's car, a blue mini coupe. That car even smelled like my grandma. She loved to wear Estee Lauder perfume, and sometimes the scent was so intense that

I knew when she had entered the room. I don't think she used too much. It was the sweet smell that would stay with me for a lifetime. With her cunning assistance, I passed the license test the first time at age fourteen. That was quite a feat!

My step-grandfather died at the end of that year. He reminded me of Uncle Scrooge. There was only one time that I remember him smiling. I was nine years old and sitting at a card table trying to learn how to play bridge. Learning to hold thirteen cards in one hand is extremely difficult. I kept dropping those playing cards that had pictures of some cars on the front. No one thought that I was too young. My grandpa would stand behind me, and if I started to play the wrong card, he would grunt. However, if I played the right card, he would smile. I persevered with bridge, and Grandpa Scrooge went back to being miserable.

After his funeral, Grandma Lee spent lots of time at our new house (not the rental, but the newly constructed house) in Virginia. We had been in that house about a year and my grandmother's visits were the highlight of our time there. The only difficulty was that I wanted my grandmother all to myself. Jealously reared its ugly head. I was forced to share her with my other brothers and sister.

Physically, Grandma Lee looked like a grandmother. She was short, round, with gray hair, and was very jolly. She was cuddly. I was growing up at a fast pace, but I could still be a kid around my grandma. That devotion and the special relationship continued between the two of us until Grandma Lee died at age eighty-nine.

Years later, I found a photo of my grandmother and this little blond-headed five-year-old holding a butterfly net standing on a front stoop. I had no memories of that time in my life, but I was smiling and was told that I loved going to visit Grandma in Iowa during the summers. We collected butterflies and pressed them in big books to add to our butterfly collection. I still have a special place in my heart for monarchs.

Life does go forward.

* * *

Burying the alcoholic did not bury the alcoholism. My mother remained the chief enabler who encouraged my behavior, good or bad, and family secrets were alive and well. I continued to babysit the two brats while my mother was dating and spent a great deal of time home alone. It was the year after we buried my stepfather, and it was also the winter after I buried my best friend, Duke, my German Shepherd that could not be replaced. Mostly black and technically a Belgian Shepherd, Duke was huge compared to other Shepherds, had the shiniest long, soft fur and eyes that penetrated when he looked at you. He never met an enemy and loved to kiss me when he knew I needed that attention. He welcomed everyone to be his friend, but I was his best "bud." Getting a new Shepherd helped ease the deep-down pain that I felt, but it was not the same. It was the first of many losses that I would experience.

My new four-legged friend, Stormy, and I did spend a lot of time together. On my fifteenth birthday, Stormy and I were sitting on the kitchen floor. It was some kind of tile that was very cold on bare skin, and Stormy was lying spread eagle, enjoying the cold temperature, on his long, outstretched legs. He kind of looked like Kermit, the frog. In front of us was the liquor cabinet, the place where mother kept the forbidden bottles. I still remember the feel of that floor after fifty years. After talking it over with Stormy, I decided to test a little white wine. It was better than the rum that I had sampled before. It was great! I felt a buzz immediately, got kind of dizzy, and wanted a whole lot more. That was the beginning of a new tragic story into alcoholism and drug addiction. That drink would change my future forever.

* * *

My mother began dating one man quite regularly, and he even came to our house for some dinners, including one Thanksgiving with the family. I started asking that enigmatic question again: "Are you my father?" I knew the answer and kept the question quietly circulating in my mind. I was hoping for a different response. Besides, this was a total stranger. It was a conversation exclusively in my imagination. No one could hear the question, and yes, no one knew the answer. The reality was the photo of someone I had never met—that man in the military uniform. That was my father. I had to keep reminding myself that he was gone, or more precisely, never there. My mother's current man was no one's father, and certainly not mine.

In the middle of all the chaos at home, I was permitted to leave the boarding school in North Carolina and attend public high school for the ninth grade. I continued to excel academically and became highly active in school. Participating in community activities was popular, and I hung around with the "in" crowd and the "nerds." I still managed to pick up Hunter and Lynn after their school every day to bring them home. Was I resentful? You betcha! I wanted to do things after school with my friends and not have the "brats" with me every day. The bottom line was that I did not want to be their mother or their father. I started rebelling and doing what I wanted to do when I wanted to do it. My mother became very frustrated with my attitude. My self-centeredness and "I deserve better" personality were emerging. My mother decided to try parenting for the first time. She started setting limits and threatening consequences. However, she had little time to really monitor my behavior and gave up trying. She continued to call me belligerent and let me self-parent.

I had already picked up a terrible habit of drinking alcohol at age fourteen when my mother was not around. Since that was often, it led to inviting other kids over to drink and on many occasions, driving drunk. I did not see this as an underage drinking problem. It was just a coping tool that seemed to work. Drinking made me popular with the other kids (so I thought). It relieved the stress and was a great way to escape into a fantasy world where I had a mother and a father that gave a damn. Many of my activities were getting riskier. Driving above the speed limit and making turns as fast as possible was a daily experience. No one stopped me so it must be OK.

About this time my mother decided to make her first big geographical cure and move to Venice, Florida. The house was sold, the furniture shipped, and the friends cut off forever. My mother never stayed in touch with anyone in Virginia, and I followed suit. Come to think of it, I am not sure she had any friends. In any case, we exchanged that past life for a new one. Having been left a substantial pool of money by my stepfather, my mother could pick and choose which part of the world she wanted to move to. She chose Venice, and I still do not know why. We lived in a rental home while our new home was being built. The new house was gorgeous. It had a swimming pool, three bedrooms, and was located on a large bay leading to the Gulf. My sister and I shared a bedroom, but only for a short time. There was a breathtaking view from every window.

Living on the water, boating became a part of everyday life. There was water skiing, testing Mercury engines for money, and pulling boats off sandbars for tips. Life seemed manageable. Feeling the wind blow through my long blond hair, bounding over the waves in the surf, and having the sun beat down on my face provided the happiness and contentment I so longed for. It brought back the memory of that Christmas holiday with my brother, Edward, when he taught me how to fish. I missed Edward and the relationship of big brother, little sister. However, I did not complain. I had my own speedboat at age fourteen and a knock-around sailboat.

You could see that money was not a problem at the time. Later the family estate from my stepfather's will would take a nosedive due to a swindling lawyer. But that did not occur for a few years down the road.

After the family moved to Florida, initially, I shared a room with my younger sister, Lynn. Physically, we were total opposites. I was average-height, 5'5", and had very blond hair. My sister was very tall for her age, seven, had long dark hair, and was "beautiful." Anyone could see that she was only my half sister. Lynn collected dolls and had hundreds of them, probably twenty. I hated all those dolls lying all around our immaculate room and insisted they be kept on Lynn's bed. At a young age, it was particularly important to me that everything had its place, be organized, and not be sloppy.

This obsessive–compulsive behavior continued through my adolescence and into adulthood. The day came when Lynn broke the unwritten rule of orderliness. She had played with her dolls and left some of them on the floor outside of the toy box and off her bed. I got a pair of scissors and cut the hair of every doll I could find. I lined them up neatly like they were holding hands on Lynn's bed. That act of terrorism got my mother's attention. The solution was to build an addition to the house so that I got my own bedroom and no longer had to share with my sister. There was no other consequence, and my temporary act of insanity was rewarded richly. My "own" room. I skated by again.

***

A move to Florida might have been a good thing if there had been some changes in the family dynamics or in my behavior. That was not the case. It was another "find a new life" for my mother that did not work.

I did make a couple of friends in Venice High School, but they were never allowed to get too close. One of those "buddies," Andrea, liked to drink beer on the weekends and be perfect during the week, which was my MO. At age fifteen, I owned a small car just like my grandmother's mini coupe. Andrea and I would drive out to the airport, hang out in the parking lot at the sleazy local bar, and look for an easy mark. For a couple of dollars, finding someone that would buy us a case of beer was not difficult. Andrea's mother worked nights so we would go back to her house, turn up the music, drink the beer, and play with her pet skunk, Stripe. Fortunately, Stripe had been de-scented, because it was entertaining to tease him and torture him as we got drunk. More than once, Stripe hid in a closet for fear of his life. Sometimes, I would drink and drive around town looking for trouble. There were no auto accidents, and the booze provided the escape from reality that I was still looking for. Being irresponsible felt good, and it was a miracle that no one was hurt or killed.

My one other good friend in high school was the smartest kid in the school. Rebecca played the first violin in the town orchestra (her father was the conductor), and she was just fun to be around. I did not have to explain things to her. She was smart. She just got it the first time around. Rebecca knew how rough things were at home for me and tried to help by inviting me to her house or attempting to include me in her family outings. Too bad that you don't pick your parents—I would have selected Rebecca's parents.

It just seemed that most kids in high school were stupid and complete "airheads." The other juniors and seniors spent their time at shopping malls, consumed entirely with fashion, hairstyle, and how they looked. I knew I was obese, ugly, and unattractive. It did not matter what I wore—I was not ever going to fit in. Sometimes it would be necessary to use the girl's restroom, and they had big mirrors above the sinks. I could not even look in the mirror because I would see just how ugly I really was. The girl in my reflection had zits, braces, and was always having a bad hair day. It was painful to look in the mirror and then return to a class with my classmates. I avoided the restrooms as much as I could. It would be years before I learned the truth: I was not only not fat, but I was anorexic and undiagnosed. My school pictures were attractive (viewed years later), and at that time, I thought they looked repulsive. My unrealistic perceptions and personal distortions would also last a lifetime. I had learned to hate myself at a young age.

Excelling in school was never enough. There was an inner drive to be the best, to be perfect for other activities. There were many choices, and I pushed myself hard. In Venice, Florida, in addition to performing on the trampoline, there was the diving team and the waterskiing squad. They were all challenging, fun, and competitive, and they involved risks. Those demanding activities attracted me like a magnet, and I gave 110 percent to each of them. I was president of the Keyette Club (a community service club). Once a week I would drive to the migrant farm out by the airport and teach the young migrant children how to read. I volunteered at the YMCA by giving trampoline lessons to eight- and nine-year-olds. I was extremely busy with a terrible self-image, continued to only have a few close friends, and knew that something was missing. I still felt alone most of the time, even in a crowd.

Every kid in high school should have a Miss Hailey. Guidance counselors are supposed to advise, console, encourage, motivate students as they transition from eighth-grade geeks to mighty seniors. Miss Hailey did that and a whole lot more. She was the faculty advisor for the Keyette Club and told me, as she probably did everyone, "My office door is always open and come see me whenever you want." It sounded like a line that I had heard from other teachers in my past, and they only mouthed the words with no sincerity or action. Well, Miss Hailey used the school pager to summon me to her office the first day of my eleventh grade, which was my first day in the new school. I kept her at arm's length for a few months, as I did not want her to see how scared and insecure I really was. She was at all our Keyette Club meetings, and I tried a new approach for me. When we were together, I would drop a little crumb of my true emotions just to see if Miss Hailey could be trusted not to tell someone else of my deep, secret feelings. In hindsight, those crumbs were more like stones that would make a path and lead somewhere. I wanted so desperately to confide in this new adult friend, but I knew if I shared with her about my sinful behaviors and some of my screwed-up thinking, that would be the end. She would surely turn me in to the principal for disciplinary action, or worse, call my mother. On the contrary, she just invited me to her office, shut the door, and told me, "You are a brilliant student, extremely talented, and can do anything you want in this world." I can hear her voice to this day. I just sat there in disbelief that someone thought that way about me. Our relationship blossomed over the next two years, and I survived high school because of Miss Hailey. I never told her that I had been sexually abused as a child or raped when I was sixteen. There was still too much guilt to bring that up, and it would be many years before I discussed anything on that topic. "Thank you, Miss Hailey."

I did date in high school, but there were no meaningful relationships, and I tended to always keep some distance. The reasons were undoubtedly valid. I knew if anyone really got to know my family or me, they would certainly not like me. They would know how different I was and would see that I was crazy from a messed-up family. Besides, I was too busy to date and was afraid of sex. That fear, I would learn, came from my abusive childhood experiences and was baggage I would carry with me for an exceedingly long time.

In between all the practicing of sports and other activities, I continued to parent my younger brother and sister. I gave them rides everywhere and took them where they needed to be. I checked up on my mother around the clock, monitored all her dating, and kept my grades on the A+ honor roll (perfect). No one recognized that this adolescent girl was driving herself into the ground and there was absolutely no suspicion of a psychological or physical illness. Was I a good actor or was no one paying attention? Miss Hailey was the only one who could see behind the mask and offer a safe place where it was OK to be me.

* * *

Summers during high school were also exciting and transcended any experiences I had lived before. Residing in Florida on the bay with a beautiful cabin cruiser parked in your backyard is a dream come true for many kids. However, it was a challenge for my family and me. My mother wanted to explore and go places, and there was only one stumbling block. She was uncomfortable and afraid to be the captain of our thirty-six-foot-long yacht. My younger brother, the only male at home, was only ten. So, I enrolled in a six-week Coast Guard Charting and Safety Procedures Course and off we went. During the summers there were two trips to the Bahamas, and most ports still remember a sixteen-year-old female in a bikini with long blond hair pulling in our big boat to their docks. The crew was my mother, who could not dock the boat with twin screws, and my ten-year-old brother, Hunter, and my eight-year-old sister, Lynn, both of whom got seasick. Captain Janet turned a lot of heads because I was exceptionally gifted at handling this yacht. We spent two full summers cruising the Bahamian Islands. Often, I would pull into a boat slip, and the dockhands would ask that question: "Where is your father?" There were a couple of human-interest articles in the local papers. Of course, with no drinking age restrictions, I was drinking my way through every island and spending way too much time in the bars with the older captains. I listened to all the sea stories and believed every word I heard. Sitting at the other end of the counter on her own bar stool was my mother. This was a prescription for trouble.

During one of those trips, my brother, Hunter, was almost murdered. The family had docked in Nassau and was staying on Paradise Island, an unfit name for what was to transpire. One of the James Bond movies had just been filmed on the island, and my mother told me to take my brother and sister over to see the site where they were shooting the movie. It was a very sweaty, hot day and no one really wanted to go. At some point, I yelled for Hunter and Lynn to come with me and go back to the boat. Hunter refused. It was a slow burning rage that came from nowhere but built up to an inferno. I began yelling for Hunter to come, now! I screamed at him like I was calling a dog on a long stretch of beach. He refused to answer, and I started to chase after him with the intent of hurting him when I caught him. This had never happened before. The anger had emerged earlier, but never the rage and feeling of being out of control. I was homicidal and wanted to kill him. He felt it; he heard it in my voice, and he hid. The hunt lasted thirty to forty minutes, and finally, I gave up. My whole body felt racked with pain, and I had never felt so emotionally spent as I did at that moment. I could not explain it and certainly could not understand it. There was a small cove next to one of the hotels, and I took Lynn and went into the water. After my body was submerged in the slightly chilly water for a good fifteen minutes, I felt the rage subside. The crisp, clear water and soft, fine sand beneath my feet were calming. Dipping my long hair in the water and splashing my face felt like an aphrodisiac. Swimming underwater produced freedom that I seldom experienced. Not only did the anger dissipate but I felt the weight of the world off my shoulders. It was the first time that I knew something was terribly wrong with me. I was different. Maybe I was crazy. I knew that I never wanted anyone to know exactly how I felt or what I had experienced. That hostility toward Hunter would fester over many years.

Lynn and I headed back to the boat. Eventually, Hunter returned to the *Simpatica*, the yacht. Not one word was said about the incident. Both Hunter and I knew that it was profoundly serious, but neither understood the deadly chase. Thirty-five years later we finally spoke about Paradise Beach and how misnamed it was on that summer day.

* * *

Sitting high on a flybridge of a thirty-six-foot cabin cruiser in the middle of crystal-blue waters with a sky-blue horizon and rolling sea before you feels magnificent. My long blond hair was blowing straight back off my face with the wind. The sun was soaking my skin, and occasionally, there was a fine mist of spray that went across my body and left some salt behind. I was in total control. I was the captain. I told every member of my family what to do and when. "Fasten those bowlines; secure those aft lines; check the fuel!" Since I was the only one who could successfully navigate or dock the boat, it was mine to command.

In good weather, navigation was uncomplicated, and I could do my very favorite pastime, fishing. I was good at it. For someone who has little or no patience, it was incredible that I was able to fish for hours, patiently awaiting results. The joy of the catch, the excitement, and the release said it all. I was in my element on the water. I was happy and did not even recognize how I felt. It was the first time that I flirted with elation and euphoria. It was an unusual emotion for me, and there was no one close that summer to support and share those feelings, to encourage the joy, or to acknowledge the happiness. My mother tried. Life was still unpredictable and exciting.

Consequently, there was more serious trouble in the Bahamas, and it was to be expected. Too many beers. I passed out and woke up naked on a deserted beach. I saw my pants about twenty feet up the beach and one tennis shoe flipping back and forth where the water met the sand. After pulling up my sandy pants and doing a thorough search of the area, I located my T-shirt up the beach. Unable to find my other shoe, I headed into the small island village. The grass huts were incredibly open, and I thought maybe I could find someone that would lend me a pair of shoes. I was flummoxed, embarrassed, and mortified to be in this situation. Perhaps someone could give me a ride to the docks. There were a couple of jeeps on the island. I tried to think of a good story, a lie that would work. I knew my attacker and blamed myself for being so stupid. I could not come up with anything believable. When your head is still spinning, you want to vomit, and your body feels like it has been run over by a truck, it is hard think up a good alibi. I did find a pair of flip-flops and walked to the docks. Flip-flops come up later in my life story.

After being raped, I just wanted to die and could not figure out a way to do it. It was the first time I thought of killing myself but not the last. Remembering only parts of the night before, I knew that I was in big trouble. I had taken the yacht to this adjacent island and still had to navigate back to Exuma Cay. I had to try and explain to my mother why I was gone all night and had not radioed my whereabouts. Being entirely hung over, the trip back was a significant challenge and would not be the first time that I had gotten into deep trouble because of my drinking.

I was an excellent captain and could typically dock the cabin cruiser in any situation with complete ease and confidence. However, when I returned to our berth at the dock, I was still foggy, definitely hungover, and did not take notice of the larger yacht that was in the next berth. Having backed up the boat into our reserved slip with as much skill as possible, the massive bang and pop noise was a big surprise. In the next slip, there was a forty-two-footer with extended outriggers for tuna fishing. I had clipped both of them with my extended outriggers. The captain of the other boat was yelling profanities, and the entire scene was chaotic. My mother rushed down to the dock to start the "4th degree" on me, as to my whereabouts the night before. The other captain was still pointing at his outriggers screaming that it was inconceivable that someone would allow a sixteen-year-old girl to handle a yacht by herself. My mother forgot about my unexplained absence and offered to pay for the damaged outriggers. The other captain quit yelling. That was not the first time my mother had bailed me out, and it would not be the last. Fortunately, the outcome of that night was mononucleosis and not something much worse, like pregnancy, HIV, or some sexually transmitted disease.

I spent the next six weeks of my senior year in high school in a hospital and the remainder of the year on a highly restricted schedule due to the mono. I continued to drink and never told anyone about the rape. I did find out later that most women do know their rapist. I had dated this English guy a couple of times. He was nine years older, talked with a British accent, was tall and attractive. Most important, he drank like I did, and his favorite was a nice, cool Heineken. He helped me feel numb and become totally vulnerable. I was an easy target. In hindsight, I was playing a dangerous game trying to be an adult in a sixteen-year-old body. I certainly did not understand sex, the consequences, or the risks. One colossal achievement during that time was my restricted diet that caused terrific weight loss, and I finally thought my body image was acceptable (five more pounds off would not hurt).

* * *

It was time for another geographic move and the whole family needed a change. I knew things were not right when I realized that there was not one friend that I would miss or be sad to leave behind, except for Miss Hailey. In fact, I was absolutely devoid of any feelings at this time and later recognized the depression that permeated my life. I started taking more risks by driving faster and taking the S-turns as tight as possible with the thought of maybe I would make it or perhaps I wouldn't. The only thing I looked forward to was getting drunk on the weekends. I did not think about the drinking part but only on the dulled feelings that resulted from being drunk or passing out. I knew that I could not be an alcoholic because I was too young.

* * *

We lived in Florida for two years and my mother was ready for a new geographic cure. Looking back on her decision to leave the United States and move to a foreign country, it was very impulsive and to a great extent, not just eccentric, but crazy. I did not know the difference. Switzerland, here we come!

After graduating from high school at the top of my class, I missed my actual graduation and was not one of the speakers, as was the tradition at the time. My mother booked the plane tickets two days before the ceremony. Very strange! Who misses their high school graduation? What is odd is that I took it all in my stride, flew to London, and drove the family to Switzerland. Just like captaining the boat, I always did the driving. Of course, that was not just any car. My mother had purchased a VW camper for the trip. The top pushed up, and when we stopped for camping, there were two double beds at each end. Space was tight with a dinette and a small stove and a miniature refrigerator in the middle. Mother could have afforded any top five-star hotel for our journey, but she opted to camp across Europe to our destination. It reminded me of our summer camping in Virginia and brought back deep thoughts about those adventures. It seemed that most of my childhood memories were very confusing, with terrific highs and depressing lows.

We began our European tour in London. I remember Big Ben, all the traffic, and Hyde Park. Driving on the left side of the road took some practice but was not that difficult except for the traffic circles. We got some real French fries, the British kind, on our walk through town and ended up on a corner in Hyde Park. There were pigeons everywhere. I never laughed so hard in my whole life. Lynn was looking up at the birds and *plop*, right on her right eye and nose. She was not amused and started crying hysterically. My mother and brother were also laughing while a perfect stranger stopped and offered Lynn a white handkerchief to wipe her face. It was a memorable moment.

There was a movie about touring Europe, called *If It's Tuesday, This Must Be Belgium*, and that described our whirlwind trip through Luxembourg, France, Italy, and finally Switzerland. My mother was anxious to get to our final destination. We would pull up to a museum, church, or some other historical spot and Mother would say the name, read something from the Michelin Guide, and announce that we were not going to visit because we were short on time. We did spend a couple of days in Paris and I found out my high school French was useless. Every time that I tried to talk to a Parisian, *en francais*, the person would look quizzical, shake their head, and say very clearly, "Ne comprend pas." We did meet a French guide who told us that the Parisians do not like Americans, and it does have something to do with the Vietnam War. I did not understand the explanation but did accept that there was a hostile attitude toward us. In any case, with all the family traveling in close quarters, we got along amazingly well and were extremely excited to start a new life in Switzerland.

* * *

It was late afternoon when we drove around a hairpin curve and drove into the Alpine valley where Gstaad was located. Immediately, Lynn, threw up in the back seat from motion sickness. It did put a damper on the moment. However, the view was majestic. At one end of the valley, there was a small airport where gliders were doing "touch and goes" and soaring through the bright blue skies. There were cotton-ball clouds dispersed over the highest mountains I had ever seen. Photos of the Alps do not do justice to the luscious green shades of endless mountains cut by more intense hunter green valleys and glistening streams traveling down from snowcapped glaciers. Amongst the trees, you could see squares of solid green that were dotted with cows and goats. Chalets sporadically appeared in the lower hills, and the two villages of Saanen and Gstaad showed clusters of stores and churches. It was the most beautiful sight I had ever experienced. We stopped the van on a turnout and tried to take it all in despite the clamoring in the back seat and my mother's insistence that we pause to let Lynn vomit outside the car.

That first summer in Switzerland was an incredible introduction to life in the Alps. We had rented a chalet close to the village and were in the process of building our new chalet a quarter of the way up a beautiful mountain, the Wispile. Gstaad is nestled between the Alps in the Bern province and looks out on the Diableret glacier. The building process was slow, but the result was majestic. Our new house had incredible views, was surrounded by pastures with Swiss cows, fields covered by wildflowers, and it was only a short walk to town. Every week we would choose a new hike, put on our backpacks, and explore the mountains and valleys at our back door. Five peaks had ski lifts, gondolas, open in the summer with a restaurant at the top of each. Learning German was a must. We were fortunate that we befriended a Swiss couple who spoke English and lived nearby. Peter and Maggie were in their late twenties and in need of work. Since Pete was a ski instructor, he was hired to cross train us and get us ready for skiing. Maggie helped with German instruction, and I really liked them both. All our long hikes ended up with a picnic lunch and a bottle of wine. Hiking boots were required, and I do remember slipping them off to put my feet in a fresh stream. I never knew my feet could feel so good. My toes were tingling and the water was crystal clear. One of our favorite walks was to Saanen to visit the Saanensee, a small pristine lake, and the local church. Who would have dreamed that I would be married in that chapel?

Very, very good or very, very bad! That description of life continued as we spent the next year in the *Sound of Music* land, complete with Julie Andrews and the Alps. Liquor flowed freely, and legal age made no difference. I was introduced to marijuana and LSD. Acid was a great way to warm up on the gondola ride to the top of the mountain. An imported German beer helped with the ski run down the slope. I was in deep trouble and did not know it. I was in a fast car in the fast lane with no seat belt.

There were long hikes with the family and long trails taken alone that were good for the soul. I was still searching but had no idea what I wanted or, more important, whom I wanted to find. There were no sand dunes, but the mountains provided the same kind of protection that I saw as a little girl in the dunes. The hay would blow and sway like the sea oats dancing in the wind. There were secret places that I could go where no one would find me. There was still that dilemma of hiding and wanting to be noticed. Several times I stole my mother's car and ran away from home. When I ran out of money (twice in Lugano, Italy), I came home. It was not until I had children of my own that I realized the fear, powerlessness, and uncertainty that I placed on my mother's shoulders.

The first fall in Switzerland my mother enrolled Hunter and Lynn in the local private school named Le Rosey. The attendees to this boarding school were very noteworthy, including lots of royalty, the Kennedy children, and other famous namesakes. The academics were second to none and the students who attended went on to top-notch, ivy league universities abroad and in the United States. There was little free time for the students, and they participated in many activities, including sports, skiing, and the arts (drama, music, and painting).

Since Le Rosey began in first grade and continued until the end of high school, many of the children grew up and matured in the four white buildings beyond the Palace Hotel. It was not unusual for the students to spend holidays and summer vacations at the school. We lived ten minutes away and I assumed that Hunter and Lynn would come home on weekends and all holidays. That was not the case. My mother wanted them to have the full experience of this exclusive school for the rich and discouraged visits home to our chalet. I did not understand this logic and just accepted that this was the way it was going to be. Hunter and Lynn had no voice in this matter and often complained of being homesick, depressed, and forgotten. I guess we all adapted. During weekends I might catch a glimpse of my brother and sister either in town or on the ski slopes. My older brother, Edward, never came to visit, and I was told that he moved to California to do his own thing.

* * *

Naturally, skiing had become a big part of my life, and it was a daily activity from October until April. Not only was I surprisingly good, but I met some competitive, crazy older kids who liked to ski hard and party harder. I was still a risk-taker, and some of my new friends thought that I was dangerous. It was that "Whatever!" attitude. I knew that I was different from my friends. I still did not allow anyone to get too close. I did take risks; I always drove too fast and played other dangerous games.

One game that I liked to play was to borrow my mother's sports car, a Lancia Flavia. I would drive through several, seven to be exact, Alpine villages to reach the Swiss capital, Bern, in the least amount of time. I would try and set new records on each attempt. Fortunately,

I never killed anyone along the way of whom I am aware. It was a treacherous game. I realized for the first time; I did not care if I lived or died.

Experimentation is typical for a teenager, but the antics that my friends and I pulled went beyond one's wildest imagination. One night we broke into a condominium that had an indoor pool and jumped in with all our ski clothing on. One girl among us even had a plaster cast on one leg. We escaped and headed straight for the hospital to get the leg reset. By some fluke of circumstance, I had left my underwear in the pool, and it had my sister's name tag sewn in the waistband. When questioned by the police the next morning, I turned to my mother, who promptly lied for me, and the entire affair was forgotten. The enabler scored again.

Skiing at night is a favorite pastime in Switzerland and usually takes place once a week, after a fondue party on top of a specific mountain. Wednesday night was the designated night, and my friends and I almost always participated. One night, we took our own alpine trail down the mountain, did not follow the ski patrol with his lighted torch, and skied close to a very steep edifice. The group made a very unhealthy decision to push a farmer's sled, commonly used to carry hay, down the mountain. The plan was to jump on board and ride on the sled. I was almost always the creative genius behind these ideas but was careful not to take credit for their outcome. In any case, as the wooden vehicle went off course and approached the cliff, everyone jumped off and avoided falling 500 feet into a steep ravine. One of the boys did break his leg, and it wasn't until the group had him in the van on the way to the hospital that I mad another discovery: I had stuck a ski pole into my upper thigh. The cold had numbed the pain, but once the heat of the van thawed out everyone, I noticed that I had blood dripping down my leg and realized what had happened:

the pole had gone two inches into my leg. Six stitches later all was well, except for the rip in my ski pants.

Escape is one word that you hear from alcoholics and drug addicts. It is not unusual to want to stop thinking, to stop feeling the pain, the emotional and mental illness that comes with alcoholism and drug addiction. I was experiencing a great deal of confusion during that first year in Switzerland, a hiatus from school in the US. I was trying to learn how to be independent, how to "fly" on my own, how to soar without crashing and having a great deal of difficulty. I was turning to all the wrong people for help. I got to know a Swiss ski instructor and thought that the girl could help me learn German, help improve my skiing (so I was the best), and help me meet new people so I could make new friends. However, it was Lydia who introduced me to my new Swiss friends, marijuana and the little sugar cubes laced with LSD. Money was not an issue, and she became my trusted dealer.

It did not matter what state or what country I lived in; I had no problem finding trouble. I was on a downward spiral into the depths of alcoholism and drug addiction. At eighteen, I rationalized my behavior by still being an experimenting adolescent and not a responsible adult. Besides, everyone drank and drugged just like I did. My stepfather had been a drunk. Everyone knew that men with long trench coats who lived on the streets were alcoholics or addicts. I had the persistent delusion that I was not that bad. It was easy for me to make the argument that I was too young and still had control of my playthings and my playmates. The problem was that deep down, I knew better. When I used drugs or drank booze, I could relate to people, be more fun to be around, and all the fears disappeared. Alcohol did become my best friend. If I were an alcoholic or an addict, so be it. Unfortunately, my moods were still so erratic. I would be on top of the world one minute (literally) and drop into deep depression the next. Something had to change.

I made the decision to go back to the States and start over by going to college. I really had no direction, but it sounded like a good thing to do. If you were an American teenager, it was expected. The Pierces were my only connection left in the States, and it had been over two years since I had seen them. Where to go? What state or geographical area competes with Switzerland? Academically, I really could go almost anywhere. Spin the bottle? Pin the tail on the map? The choice was very scientific. I decided to follow an old boyfriend from high school and go where he went. My mother had little input, and there was no one else to consult. I had been making all my own big decisions since I was thirteen, and this was one more to add to the list.

You attract a great deal of attention when you are the only freshman with Switzerland as your home address, and attention is something that I still craved. However, all the same rules applied. Don't let anyone get too close; excel in all your classes to prove you are worth something; pretend to be happy all the time because that's what people want; and above all, do anything to stay out of the black hole. The hole was not like the one that Alice fell in. It was dark, cold, spinning, and had no bottom. If I started to sink into that deep abyss called depression, I knew that all those feelings of loneliness, fear, guilt, and hopelessness would return.

College was an alcoholic's dream, and the trick was learning to pace yourself from weekend to weekend. I managed to get through my first year without incident and flew back to Switzerland in May of 1970 to visit my family. This date is important. Not only was I nineteen at that time, but we were engaged in the Vietnam War; there were armed security guards at all the airports, and there did not seem to be much talk of world peace. I started singing "Bye Bye American Pie" like everyone else. The world was not a happy or hopeful place.

My mother picked me up at the airport in her gray Volvo sedan and immediately asked me if I would drive. Some things never change. It is about a three-hour drive to the chalet from the airport, and only four or five words were exchanged the first hour of the trip. Finally, my mother broke the silence with the proverbial question: "What's wrong?"

Many people describe turning points in their lives as earth-shattering events that turned their whole life around 360 degrees, some for the better and, indeed, some for the worse. When you are close to someone and they die, it can positively influence how you think, feel, and act in the future. When an individual survives a terminal illness, there is a profound effect on the survivor and those close to the diagnosed person. It is incredible that an average lifespan is eighty years and it only takes a few minutes or a few hours to alter the course of that life forever. The life-changing events list goes on and on. But what happened to me during that drive in Switzerland on a bright, beautiful day in May is not categorically listed as a lifetime experience that can change your entire outlook on life. It did!

*　*　*

"What's wrong?" my mother asked in a shakier tone. I decide to answer her honestly by telling her that I just did not want to live anymore. I had broken up with my boyfriend and planned to drop out of school. "I do not know how to live. If I only had a father to talk to; someone to hold me (my mother never touched me); a parent that I could get advice from. I need a father." I waited for her standard reply: "You think that I am a bad parent?" There must have been desperation in my voice, and it did not take a shrink to spot my deep depression. My emotional affect was flat. I was not facing my mother. There was no eye contact. You could cut the silence with a knife.

* * *

I had lost a lot of weight, and my clothes were hanging off me. I held the steering wheel in a vice grip like the car might just run away. My mother said that she had something to tell me that might not only change our relationship but my outlook on life forever. She had my full attention. I asked her, "Are you going to have me committed?" There was more silence.

Finally, my mother said, "You do." "I do what?" *What was she talking about?* She went on to explain: "The military man in the photo was not your father. Your father is alive and well and lives in Rhode Island. You were conceived out of love. Bruce King could not have any more children; he did not want any more children, and he took care of that himself."

I whipped the car off the road onto the shoulder and stared at my mother like I was seeing her for the first time. "What!" I was shocked. No, I was perplexed and shocked.

Chapter 3: Learning to Fly

Flying a Cessna in 1964 was not as difficult as it sounds. You strap yourself in, give the little bird plenty of gas, gently pull back the wheel until the nose comes up, and leave the runway for a specific destination. Fortunately, you have a copilot when you are learning to do this who tells you the order of things and just how much of what to do when. Here I was, soaring through my adolescence, my twenties, and early adulthood with no copilot, no instructor, and no parachute. I had to spread my wings and learn to fly solo.

When you have been lied to all your life, you tend to believe no one. My mother had just dropped the bomb. "Your father is alive. He lives in Newport, Rhode Island. Yes, you are nineteen, and he has only seen you once when you were two, but he does know he is your father. Oh, he is also famous."

She was telling me this like she was describing buying milk at the local store and it was no big deal. Being suicidal at the time, I was not quite sure how to react to the news. Some of that old rage was returning, but there was also an unwillingness to accept what I was hearing. My mother had lied to me repeatedly. Why believe her now? This news was just too convenient, too easy to manufacture at a time of crisis. I was threatening to kill myself, and my mother had no idea how to stop me. I decided to crash our car, but we were not moving. We were still standing idle on the shoulder of the highway. I was at an all-time low and my mother could not help me soar through this one. But, yeah! Produce a father for me? Maybe that was the best she had. Was it working?

I was trying to get my bearings. We were not moving and were parked on the side of the road outside of Bern on the way back from Zurich airport. I was in the driver's seat. You could see the Alps sticking their heads up from the clouds in the distance. The view was incredible and did distract me for a few seconds, four seconds. Sitting in the car staring straight ahead, there was dead silence. Finally, I told my mother to tell the truth, the whole truth, and as they say, nothing but the truth. I was not smiling. I still had an iron grip on the steering wheel, and I was not letting go. The motor was still running, and I was still looking straight ahead over the dash. Slowly, I pulled forward, and we drove in silence back to the chalet and parked in the driveway in the perfect position, perpendicular to the garage. With a deadpan expression, I turned to my mother and told her we were going to call this new "daddy" immediately. Within five minutes he was on the line and confirmed what I had been told. I was nineteen years old. Unbelievable! Now, the next question was, "Are you sure that you are my father?" It turned out that he was a big muckety-muck in the Navy, was married, and had five other children from his current and only marriage. I had no idea where I fit into this picture. Or did I want to fit?

*　*　*

In our society, and worldwide, it just is not that unusual to be a sperm-bank child or to be born out of wedlock. Many women and men can certainly relate to this situation and might be searching for their father, or as they say today, their biological father. It was all the ongoing lies that complicated my story. First, I had been told that my stepfather was my "real" father. Following that deception, I was led to believe that a dead Navy doctor was "really" my biological father. Now, I was being told that none of that was the truth. My biological father was someone else, not shown in any photographs, and in fact, was someone else's father too. My mother tearfully confessed about the one-night affair that she had and how sorry she was about her big mistake. A mistake is when your pencil slips on the paper, and you use the eraser to fix it.

Just observing her part of "the" phone call was revealing. She got him, my real father, on the line and declared that she had told me the truth. Except, it did not sound like a confession. There appeared to be no guilt, no admission to adultery, or any compassion during the revealing phone conversation. The attitude from my mother could be summed up as: "Let the relationship go where it may. It's really no big deal."

After the phone call, she defended her position by stating that she really was not sure about my lineage until she found a life insurance policy that had the name Janet Hollins listed as the beneficiary. Admiral Hollins was the only explanation. So, her first husband, the man in the uniform, knew about the affair from the get-go. It was all very confusing, and I was just not sure who or what to believe.

* * *

The question "Who am I?" is often defined by who our parents happen to be. However, not being able to choose our parents can make genetics, behaviors, relationships a big challenge. We know that stepparents, blended families, and single-parent homes are much more prevalent today than when we were children. But today, just like yesterday, children need to be told the truth at an age appropriate to the circumstance or situation. This is my opinion, and I am sticking by it.

*　*　*

Several days after the initial phone call to confirm the truth, I received a letter from my new father, signed, "Love, Daddy." It would be eleven more years before I would meet my father for the first time. I was drunk on this special occasion and have little recall of the entire event. Every day from that moment in the car in Switzerland until that fateful first dinner in Washington, D.C., over a decade later, I played a movie scene in my head. All of us have watched these scenes on *Unsolved Mysteries*.

Parent and child reunions are a prevalent theme on that show. These episodes end with the child or adult-child who has been searching for his or her lost parent, running into their arms with astounding joy and happiness. The story flips the coin, and the parent is joyous and free to have finally located their long-lost child. Everybody is smiling and full of happiness and gratitude that they have finally found each other. In my life, I expect no less of a production and outcome. A stunning young girl with long, flowing blond hair runs across the lobby of an expensive five-star hotel into the outstretched arms of her father, her "real" father and they embrace for the very first time. She does not ask him questions, but proudly announces, "You are my father." The search is complete. I finally reach a significant destination on my roads to life.

If we rewind to reality, there was no happy rendezvous. On the contrary, there was resentment and a wall of anger that did not come crumbling down. "Why? Why? Why did you lie to me? Why didn't you come visit me? How could you pretend that I didn't exist?" Those are the questions that I wanted to be answered. *My mother could not be honest, but why couldn't he?* Over the next decade, the answers would be revealed.

* * *

Back to that second summer in Switzerland, I was extremely stressed out and decided to return to college early and attend summer school. It was a tranquil escape from the family, from my mother, and I had met someone special, a boy who acted like a man. He told me that he loved me. I decided that attention was love and love was getting attention. This definition would be under scrutiny for the rest of my life.

* * *

Relationships to this point had all been very superficial because of my rule to not allow anyone to get too close emotionally. I had felt used by boys or men. Indeed, I had been sexually abused as a child and raped as an adolescent. Trust would be an issue for many, many years. Alcohol played a huge role in that teen rape, but I did not see the connections until years later. Lacking trust and flying solo were the only way I was willing to go at that point in time. However, the turn of events in Switzerland in discovering that I had a father and the total alienation of my mother influenced my relationships with others. Not only did I feel entirely deceived, but now I felt abandoned by my father. Every effort that I made to contact him was met with significant resistance. He told me that he had a real family, a wife and five children, four daughters and one son, and that I was nowhere in the picture. He commanded that I do not call him or write him at home because our "arrangement" was to be kept secret. I was not a long-lost daughter. I was an arrangement. I was given a post office box to write to, and unbelievably, he did write back. I was told never to call him for fear that someone else might answer the phone. In other words, that ugly word "shame" became a part of my new personal inventory. Something must be very wrong with me that my own father felt the way he did. My dream scene of outreached arms had become very distorted. I did not feel worthy of a good relationship with a man. With anyone.

I felt "unclean," like damaged goods that no one would want. These feelings were complicated because there were times of change where I believed great things were possible. I started having manic days (my brain was on fire) when I first started college, and I felt I could accomplish great things. My thoughts were grandiose and secretly, I believed that I was destined for greatness. I learned to speak German and French in Switzerland and was fluent in both. For the first time, my studies in college were challenging, and sometimes I would stay up all night to do the work necessary to get the top grades I wanted and deserved. I had to change my drinking and drugging habits to accommodate my new study habits and social interactions. Sleeping and eating were important if I was going to learn how to stay healthy and excel in this new college curriculum. Confusion, feeling "up" one moment and "down" the next, made college life extremely difficult. I learned to self-medicate, and that is how I met my future husband.

* * *

"You will really like this guy." I had heard that many times and had repeatedly been disappointed. Blind dates were definitely overrated. However, my defenses were down. I was trying to orchestrate this new arrangement with my new father and figure out where I fit in the scheme of things. Often, I was depressed and was not overly excited about starting my second year of college. A blind date to a frat party sounded just as good as doing my laundry. I gave in and agreed to meet this couple and this "fantastic" guy later that night.

Some research studies suggest we pick out a mate who resembles or has the personality of our parent. A girl looks for all the character traits of her father and searches out a boyfriend who exhibits similar behavior. All the research in the world was not going to change my dilemma. I did not really know my father. So, I threw fate to the wind and took this new guy hostage.

The original attraction was not just his good looks—he was also extremely intelligent. He was pledging for the top fraternity, and he could carry on a decent conversation. He did not seem overly impressed that my home address was Switzerland. He was an entrepreneur on campus as he sold shots of whiskey out of his briefcase. *What more could one ask for?*

The first date was a semi-blind date in that I had scoped him out earlier and liked what I saw. It was a double date with a girl from my home room and we decided to attend a fraternity party that had a free open bar and a list of drinks they were offering. It was an alcoholic's nirvana. I suggested to my date, Wes, that we start at the top of the list and just go down the menu. I was also the first one to pass out. The two boys, who were also drunk, carried me back to my dorm room. I hugged the toilet bowl all night and was sweating something that smelled and resembled Vaseline. I found out a couple of days later that all my black and bruise spots came from being repeatedly dropped by my transporters.

However, it was love at first sight and the "shot seller" and I began a relationship that would span fifteen years. From that prophecy-filled first date until the very end, I was still searching. I certainly could not say I had found the image of my father because there was none. After my first encounter with my father over ten years down the road, I knew that this boyfriend and my father had nothing in common.

Movies like *Hope Floats* are what movie-goers flock to see. Engagements, weddings, remarriages, blended families, stepparents, and even adopted children that fare extremely well are the box-office hits. My story is obviously not a movie and would not fill the theater unless we rewrite *Cinderella* to include huge calamities, devastating trials, tribulations, hitting bottoms, and finally the fairy princess ending. I would never find my pearly slippers or flip-flops, as had happened to me years before. Prince Charming would have to be an incredible recovering alcoholic on his way to an AA meeting, who has a hot date with Cinderella, and brings her nothing but genuine love and happiness. We don't like to rewrite fairy tales, and I was no exception. I expected a great deal from my first serious relationship and had no way of knowing how poor health, my alcoholism, and my relationship with his family would influence that outcome. In fact, that was my major problem. I still liked to make plans, but I was always planning the result and was time after time disappointed. It would be years before I discovered that I just do not have that much control. At some point, it is better to throw the future to the wind and let it blow where it may. Trying to manipulate people and things is just plain unproductive. What is worse is trying to do the same thing over and over the same way and expecting different results. After all, that is the definition of insanity. It was just stupid, "stinkin' thinkin'" when you look at my past and all the unexpected results. Back to the college campus.

* * *

Wes and I began dating exclusively and decided to go to Vienna, Austria, for an educational experience. Our college had a reciprocal studies abroad program. This would be a joint venture for my sophomore year and Wes's junior year. However, I returned to Switzerland the summer before to see my foreign friends, visit with my mother, and check up on my younger brother and younger sister. I had not seen my older brother in years and heard that he was still living in California. There had not been many family get-togethers, and there was minimal contact with Edward. After all, he was only my "half" brother now, and that seemed to make him less important. In fact, I did not have any "full" siblings. When I counted all the halves, I had three half brothers, five half sisters, and no whole anything. None of my siblings that I grew up with knew about the Admiral (that is how I referred to my biological father). None of the Admiral's offspring knew about me. It was one big family secret.

* * *

From the onset, that summer visit to Switzerland was very disappointing. My mother had leased out my bedroom to another young girl and forgot to tell her oldest daughter, me. Furthermore, the tenant was a lesbian and was expecting her lover to join her soon. I had never met a gay person and made assumptions that were way off the mark. I would learn more about her choices in later life and just had to accept that Jill was different. So was I, and it was still difficult to let her into my family. I liked her, and that threatened my own self-image. Did that mean that I was gay? I had never had any sexual feelings toward a woman, but I learned that summer not to discount that it could happen.

We did not need the money. Why rent out my bedroom? What was going on? Our Swiss chalet had been turned upside down and into a modern brothel. My mother was still dating but was not involved in any serious relationships. Men would come and go on a regular basis. It was difficult to not be judgmental and rate the male visitors after they left. Her choice of men was about a 4 or a 5 on a scale of 1 to 10, and I was generous.

The feelings were mutual. My mother had plenty of criticism for the man in my life, whom she had not even met. The other major complaint that I heard was how I had gotten too skinny (you cannot win) and how little time I was spending with the family. Truthfully, I would have lived anywhere but there that summer, given a choice.

If I forgot to mention Transcendental Meditation, now is the time. My mother was holding TM meetings at the chalet twice a week. It was the touchy, feely thing that came out of California, and the facilitator was a complete phony who charged exorbitant fees for his services. He tried to put the moves on me even though he was twelve years my senior. It was a good reason to go to town or take a solo hike away from the whole scene. However, you can find humor in most situations if you look for it.

During one of those meditation sessions, the TM guru, Michael, introduced the importance of touch. To illustrate the concept, he placed his hands squarely on a woman friend of my mother's. He was holding her voluptuous breasts firmly in his hands. With horror, the woman screamed for him to "move his hands." Much to the surprise of the victim and the other participants, the TM leader proceeded to move his hands in a circular movement, moving each breast with every motion. His comment was: "You told me to move my hands, and that is what I did." Everyone was appalled, and I just broke out laughing and left the room. TM did not survive in Gstaad, Switzerland.

I did get involved with someone that summer, and we even "hooked up," as the kids say today. It led to a hot and heavy sexual encounter in the sauna. I was supposed to be meeting Wes in the fall for our study abroad year in Vienna, Austria. The two of us had even discussed marriage, so it did feel like I was cheating in the relationship. It was very confusing. That contributed to my recklessness, low self-esteem, and constant drinking and drugging. After telling Steve, the summer fling, about Wes, Steve said that he didn't really give a f*** and our sauna dates continued. Why not? I was paying for most of our dates, and Steve was not worried about commitment because he did not want any. After a summer that had the highs and lows of a new chapter in my life, the fall arrived, and I was off to Vienna for college and Wes. It only took three weeks, and I left Wes and the University of Vienna.

By this time, my family home bedroom was free, and I returned to the chalet in Switzerland. Hunter and Lynn were back in boarding school. The question, "Are you my father?" had been answered and yet, I felt totally lost. I did not understand why my mother waited until I was nineteen to tell me the truth. When I asked her to explain, there was a long pause, and she said, "The longer that I waited to tell you, the harder it got. I was afraid that you would be upset, and my greatest fear was that you would leave me forever." Duh!

The poor communication with Mother, the total confusion about relationships, fear of suicide, and what to do about school were serious problems. Something had to break.

* * *

It was ski season, and Christmas just flew by. New Year's Eve, I had a date with Steve, and we were back in the sauna. Slightly before the New Year was toasted, I made a significant decision. I needed to see Wes one more time before I totally trashed the promise of a life together and wrote him off entirely. I left ten minutes later and drove to Zurich airport. Impulsivity was one of my character defects. I called Wes and told him on what flight I would be arriving and to please meet me there. As soon as I reached Vienna and saw him on the tarmac, my heart was in his hands. I felt unconditional love for him that I had never felt for any human except my Grandma Lee. This was the man I was going to marry. Fortunately, Wes felt the same way. We boarded the train headed for a small ski resort with a funny name, Puchberg am Schneeberg.

Our plan was just to get married, finish out Wes's college semester in Vienna, and go back to the States to start a life and complete our schooling. The plan seemed perfect and even sounded more like my "Cinderella" story. Unfortunately, or by divine intervention, no one would marry us without written parental consent because of our age. One must be twenty-one years old to marry in Austria or Switzerland or have written parental consent. Both Wes and I were only twenty. First, I called my mother and asked her to wire-transfer the consent. She refused. She said that she could get a wedding together in four weeks if we would come back to Switzerland and get married in a church near her home. This wedding was going to be all about my mother. Why was I surprised? Wes's parents were even more direct. "Hell, no! We will not send anything, but we will fly over to Switzerland and you damn well better get married." It was not exactly what we had planned, but the arrangement worked, and the wedding was the first time in my life that I did feel like a fairy princess.

Before my bridal appearance in the church, I had to walk up a stone walkway outside from the car to the front door. Hunter was giving me away. He was my escort to get me up the path and into the church. Big problem. It was snowing, cold, icy, and both of us had on dress shoes with very slick soles. For every step we made forward, we slipped back two. We were not making any progress and broke out laughing hysterically. It took ten minutes of organ music for my mother to figure out that there must be a problem. How ironic was it that Hunter was not only giving me away in the service but that it was he and I who were sharing the last funniest moment in my single life? I never loved my younger brother more than that day.

After the wedding (I have no recall of the ceremony), there was a limousine to whisk us off to Lausanne for our honeymoon. Having champagne for the two-hour ride was a mistake, and we were both plastered when we arrived at our dream hotel, the Palace. The monumental "wedding night" had to be postponed. I indeed was not a virgin, so it was no big deal.

Returning to Vienna was difficult. I was bored, not being in school and having the whole day to do nothing except wait for my new husband, Wes, who was attending classes. I did not know what to do. I was used to a frantic lifestyle, and there was no chaos and there was too much time to think. I was writing letters to my new-found father, but it would still be ten years before we would meet. Of course, he had been invited to the wedding, but he did not send a regret or show up. There were letters from the Admiral that played an important part in my story, and some will be shared later in my adventure through life.

Since my new husband and I would be spending the next four months in Vienna, which allowed Wes to complete his junior year abroad, it was up to me to stay busy and not go stir-crazy. Vienna is a large European city with lots of beautiful parks in and around the suburbs. I found all of them. On the weekends, we would go to one of the larger parks, the Prater, a favorite. We did one of the things that we did best—drink wine. Once I had a buzz, Wes would get us on the right trolley, and we would head back to our apartment to make love, which is the other thing that we did quite well.

Spring break arrived and we took the train through the beautiful Alpine passes back to Gstaad. The snow was falling in flakes the size of maple leaves, and Wes's mustache had little crystalized ice drops sticking to it when we exited the train. Besides looking like a scene out of *Frosty the Snowman*, it was extremely cold and just getting to my mother's chalet was a challenge. The taxi took us up the mountain as far as it could muster and then we climbed on foot. The homecoming was sweet, as my mother had made a "Welcome Home" sign and she was legitimately glad to see us. We were there for two days and the shit hit the fan.

Peter and his fiancée were getting married the week we arrived. Peter was one of our Swiss ski buddies and his father owned the local hardware store. He threw a huge bachelor's party where Wes got drunk, tried yodeling on top of a table, and fell and broke his collar bone. Meanwhile, back at the chalet, mother had lost her sweetness and was irritable and bored. She announced that the cold, snowy weather was keeping her homebound and she felt like a recluse. Her impulsivity and her eccentric tendencies took over. Within twenty-four hours of rescuing Wes from the hospital, with a bandaged collar bone, my mother had planned and began executing a vacation from Switzerland to the Bahamas for the three of us and my younger brother and sister who were still in Swiss boarding school. Who packs up their family and leaves a ski resort in the prime ski season because she is restless? Let the fun begin!

The plan was to fly to Nassau and then charter a sea plane to ferry us to Compass Cay in the Exumas. In other words, we would revisit the island where I lost my virginity in my adventuresome adolescence. Vacationing on a remote island without a boat is sort of like visiting

Pike's Peak to ascend without hiking boots. However, we did have a blow-up life raft. While balanced on one of the tippy pontoons of the sea plane, I did manage to inflate the six-man raft. With four large duffle bags and five people, we paddled (folding paddles) to the dock and began the most amazing escapade in our lives.

First, Wes was still wounded. He had stitches following his collar bone surgery and a first aid dressing that required a daily changing. Sand did not contribute to Wes's well-being. I forgot to mention that two of the duffle bags contained two tents, two tarps, and camping equipment and supplies for two weeks. My mother's plan of action was to set up camp on the beach, put on our bikinis, and snorkel every day on the reef. She did not include the sand fleas. Night one was a disaster. We were all getting bitten and Wes seemed to be allergic to every flea. His incision did not fare well. Fortunately, for all of us, we met Hester Crawford.

There are only two houses on Compass Cay. The clubhouse that housed the local bar, the only bar, and maintained the marina, and the hexagon-shaped cottage that sat high on the rocks at the opposite end of the cove where we were camping. By day two, Wes was in dire straits, fresh water was a problem, and we were all miserable. The only relief was head for the sea, and it was not that warm in March. There was this old woman walking down the beach and quite a sight with her big floppy hat, flip-flops, and cut-off jeans. She approached and asked if we would like to visit her house for a cup of hot tea. Within the hour, we had met Hester and were all gathered on her large screened porch. The view was magnificent and so was she. When she heard about the sand fleas, Wes's stitches, and our lack of water, she invited us to move our camp to her porch. My mother was an immensely proud woman with a huge ego, and she balked at the invitation. She did not want to admit to her lack of proper planning or her incompetent nurse's training, which was thirty-five years earlier. She only completed one semester and dropped out of the medical program. Hester was so gracious and convinced my mother that this would be good for her, as she sometimes was very lonely since her husband died. In other words, we would be doing her a favor. Smart woman.

We moved the camp that afternoon and learned the story of Hester Crawford. Her husband had written the song "Over the Wild Blue Yonder," and she had built her house overlooking one of the most beautiful white sand coves in the world from the royalties that she received from the song. She was a crusty broad and enjoyed her isolation until we descended upon her. Wes healed and the rest of us survived with the help of Hester. The sea plane returned eight days later, and we reversed the process by inflating our life raft and boarding the plane. The pilot flew over Hester's cottage, tipped his wings, and we all waved farewell. Back to Nassau, Geneva, and finally Gstaad. No one will forget that vacation and it did make us stronger. Wes and I headed back to Vienna and some sense of normalcy. I still had to complete my time as a newlywed. We had two more months to live in an incredible gorgeous city and I described it as completing a jail term. Why was I so discontent and not grateful for the opportunities we had been given? Wes asked the same question in a different way. What was wrong with his new wife?

The semester came to a close, and it was time to go home to Pennsylvania to set up our house, enroll in college, and get Wes into law school. He had done exceptionally well in his law board exams, so we were optimistic that he would get accepted. His intellect was still one of the primary reasons I was attracted to him. I was proud of him, but almost like a piece of property. The love was there, but I was extraordinarily codependent, and my entire life revolved around him. I had to have the perfect house, the best-looking lawn and garden on the block, and the right friends. The drinking slowed down, and I actually did make some new friends—law school wives and neighbors around our house. Making that house a "home" was much more difficult. I knew one thing: I did not want this home to be anything like the places where I grew up. I had just become an adult. Not only could I vote, but I could drink legally. That was funny.

Comparing my first new home to my mother's many waterfront homes, expensive chalets, villas, casas or "whatever" was impossible. Being an adult meant being fiscally responsible too. It was time to talk about money.

* * *

My stepfather had a hugely successful construction and development company when he died. He left my mother with enough money that she would never have to work again, and she could spend money recklessly and not feel a pinch. The message that I got was that money was not anything you should ever worry about and if it was there, spend it. The whole family expended nicely and became used to a lifestyle that few enjoy. There were some checks and balances on the bank accounts. The executor of the estate had his hands full with my mother's spending, and he ended up pocketing more than his share. However, the money continued to flow, and all the kids had very handsome trusts that provided for quality education, trips to the Bahamas, brick houses, and $200 jeans from Gstaad. In short, I would never have to work either, if I watched my personal spending. I ignored that part.

When it came time for Wes and me to settle down in a home of our own, I had a difficult time accepting our lower standard of living. It never crossed my mind that we were twenty-one years of age and able to buy a house, put Wes through Law School, and travel when we felt like it. There was no gratitude because I did not know how the other half lived. How did people who worked full-time and still struggled financially stay happy? My attitude was still focused on my mother and comparing our lot in life with hers. After all, she owed me for all those lies growing up, or so I thought.

The best thing about our new home was that there was an ocean between her Swiss chalet and our place. It was a lovely little brick house with nothing in it except books and more books. It probably resembled most new couples' first house, but I wanted it to be unique, to be decorated with our tastes, and be a place I did not want to run away from. The spending did get out of hand more than once. The credit cards maxed out, and I would just call the attorney or my mother to bail us out like she had done all my life. In fact, the only relationship that my mother and I had, at this time, focused on money.

Wes's family lived on the Main Line, outside of Philadelphia, and pretended to be wealthy. They had nothing, gave us nothing, and continuously reminded Wes that he was a kept man. Wes's pride was an issue, and his ego was bruised many times during those first years of marriage. It was time for a change and wow, were we blessed!

Chapter 4: Spreading My Wings

Absolute joy describes my reaction to the news that I was pregnant. After all, I had lots of practice parenting my younger brother and sister, and I wanted a baby. I knew that we would have the perfect family. My mother invited herself for the big moment, but I was glad to get the help. I sent the Admiral an announcement, and he did respond. In fact, once I received that congratulatory letter, we began routine writing of letters that continued until his death. I kept each one of them in a red plastic notebook, and I was secretly proud of my father's accomplishments that spanned the globe. I learned that he really was famous and had a celebrated career in the Navy and after he left the military. I wished that I could have shared my secrets with someone. It was time to look at those early letters and try to get some perspective on this relationship.

June 1969: The First Letter

"Dear Janet… Life has many experiences, both good and bad, but as we mature and see it in a broader perspective, our values and ideas change in many ways. First I want you to know I loved your mother and you are the offspring of a very deep love…. There was one resolve I made with your mother and that was you were never to suffer in any way for our actions…. Our secret was one that had to be kept for many reasons for the world is a cruel place in many ways and there were many other people involved…. I have thought about you for many years and now we will have an opportunity to know each other.... Unfortunately I leave for Japan Sunday and will be in the Far East for a while but intend to come to Europe real soon and hope to come see you or meet you in Europe.... We have so much to catch up on and I do so want you to be happy...."

A long poem was included in that first letter, and the Admiral described himself as a romantic, a descendant of Percy Shelley, and a pragmatic in other ways. He ended the letter by stating:

"... Hope this letter gives you as much pleasure as it gives me in writing to you. I hope you know you are loved and that I will do anything for you I possibly can. Take care of yourself and kiss your mother for me. Love, Daddy"

February 1971

"My dearest Janet... My return to New York found your message about your wedding. Fate prevented me from being there, but I know I would have been if it had been possible.... I will come see you when you tell me where you will live.... Marriage is not easy at best but just remember that love and understanding will assist man times. Marriage is not just the sex side of life, but it carries a burden of many other responsibilities to both parties. There are so many things a father can say on the subject. If one were to describe love with one word, it would be sacrifice.... I could go on for days and probably will when I see you. Love, Matt"

January 1972

"Dear Janet: Here in snow-covered Istanbul and going back to Ankara, Turkey....I definitely will surprise you and show up in Gstaad. Can't give you any specifics but you may be sure it will happen....I have so many things I want to do but haven't done in my busy life....

Hope to really study and write which I always have loved....This is just a quick note to say I am delighted to hear all is well now and wish you a happy New Year and to say I was delighted with 1971 and that you are my daughter....Love, Matt"

March 1972

"Dear Janet...I was distressed we couldn't get together in Vienna but fate wasn't very kind to me and I do have to do my job for they pay me an awful lot of money. I still love your mother and do dream we will get together and hope it can by soon....Up until 1968 I had been to every war including Southeast Asia so must comment on that for it is uppermost in everyone's mind....The so called Pentagon papers are all the talk these days. Why are they misleading? Because they leave out so much....It is a privileged thing to be an American Citizen and now that 18-year-olds can vote maybe the voice of youth will be heard. I have been all over the world and say this is the only land for me. Fromm Kabul to Melbourne, Capetown and the Congo to Helsinki, they are all fascinating and I go many other places but this is my land....When you come to talk to me, be prepared. I would love to discuss so many things with you and tell you so many other things. I can't wait....When you see your mother kiss her for me. Love, Dad"

April 1972

"Dear Janet:...Be intellectually curious about everything not just a specialty or something you like. Discipline your mind and increase your mental capacity in every way you can. You can be an achiever in your own right. I know. What shall I do? I am going back to school and will probably wind up as a professor at Harvard or some other university....The whole world is before you, there for the taking, with only yourself to be the catalyst to decide what you want to do and learn about it be it business, history or archeology....There is going to be no inner light or someone to lead you by the hand. The world is cruel and heartless and many times we are our own worst enemy....I have been in the Orient and Persia most of the recent months....I have an office in Tokyo and will be there on business....All the swish people go to Gstaad and so I am not with the in crowd....Give my love to your mother. She is such a doll. Maybe I should just go and be the houseboy or the butler. Take care of yourself. Much love, Matt"

July 1972

"Dear Janet: Just a short note to tell you hello and that I loved your letter....Have a meeting in Hawaii this coming week but will be back shortly and I hope on my way to you to stop and say hello.... Still haven't really decided on Harvard or the Navy College or a bit of both. I haven't really had time to really try my hand at writing. Being a descendant of Shelley I should be able to do a bit....I miss the sea out here in Middle America (St. Louis). Guess I have salt in my veins. I will give you a call on the phone to say hello. Love, Dad"

December 1972

"My dear Janet, ...At the moment I am in our little beach house in Florida. It is a relief to see the ocean again....As industry makes one retire when 65, I must leave this month. I am not really 65 but it is hard to change one's age back but then it really makes no difference. I did have to fudge my age by 2 years to enlist in the Navy when I was 15 so I guess I am stuck with it....Do you have a telephone?...I will be in Washington in January and will try to drive up to Pennsylvania to see you. I am dying to see you. Have a Merry Christmas! Love, Dad"

December 1973

"I will move to Washington in the spring. I finished my first five years in civilian life and now can do what I want with 2/3rds of my time....I enjoyed running the International Operations for the company and have seen much more of the world in recent years than I really needed....I still intend to get to Switzerland....Time will be more available now than before so I should make it. Kiss that grandson for me. Love, Dad"

The letters became less frequent from both of us as the Admiral was moving cross country and I began my next journey into motherhood.

Hands down! Being pregnant, giving birth, and nurturing babies were the high points of my entire lifetime. Fortunately, the pregnancies were uneventful, relatively easy, and very healthful, physically and mentally. I stopped doing drugs while I was pregnant and reduced my alcohol consumption to zero. I exercised, took Lamaze classes, joined the La Leche League and waited patiently for the "big moment."

It was a Friday afternoon, tea-time, and I was reading some baby book on the living room sofa. This was one of 22 books that I had read about babies. I wanted to be prepared. My mother and Wes, my husband, were occupied with stuff that they did and no one seemed to react when I announced that "my water just broke and the contractions are pretty strong." They both looked at me with that now-what stare until I suggested strongly that we all head to the hospital. The next few moments should have been part of a soap opera. Wes was yelling that he had to make his sandwich and pack his bag for the big event. He had learned about this in the Lamaze classes to survive the long labor. My mother volunteered to make his sandwich but could not find the mustard. I reminded both of them that I needed to get to the hospital now.

Prepared for a ten-hour first labor, my first son came into the world after only three hours of manageable contractions. "He's beautiful!" It is all I could say as I held him for the first time. My smile said it all. This was the happiest day; the most wonderful moment of my entire life. George was not only my first born, but I knew that I had finally done something right, something "perfect" in my eyes. He had blond hair (just enough), gorgeous brown eyes, and fat little cheeks. At eight pounds and fourteen ounces, George was a big baby and hungry twenty-four hours a day. That was fine with me because I did not want anyone to take him back to the nursery and was quite elated to hold him forever, one hour at a time. On the second day at the hospital, the nurse brought my new son to me, and he had scratched his nose with his fingernail. Even though it was cute, it upset me. I never wanted him to experience any hurt, pain, or discomfort for as long as he lived. That was a full-time job and proved to be impossible. The pediatric nurse trimmed his fingernails, and the new Mom and baby George went home the following day. The nursery at our home was picture perfect, and the white bassinet was right next to our bed. It seemed like every action by my mother or Wes, his new Dad, created a reaction in George and both parents agreed that he was not only gorgeous but brilliant. It would be great fun to spoil our first child forever.

That bond endured until the present day with me, his Mom, but unfortunately, ended abruptly with his Dad. Our divorce (nine years later) trashed the relationship George had with his father. It was impossible for either one of them to ever repair the damage.

George was a well-traveled baby and crossed the Atlantic Ocean four times before he was age two. At six weeks, he went to visit his grandmother in Switzerland, wore Swiss lederhosen, nursed on an Alpine chairlift, and hiked up and down several mountains in a backpack. He was held and cuddled by Julie Andrews when she came to visit my mother. George was indeed a miracle baby, and it was a Swiss doctor who made it all possible.

When Wes and I decided to have a baby, I was devastated to discover that I had not ovulated and pregnancy was very unlikely. However, an assertive fertility specialist in Geneva, Switzerland recommended ninety days of daily hormone injections, and it worked. Our son was living proof that miracles do happen and something spectacular could be the result of trials and tribulations. The word was hope. I had never believed in that word or thought it would ever be part of my life, my future.

Wes was finishing up Law School, and we were raising our son with the expectation of having three more children just like him. A girl would be lovely. That decision confirmed my career choice to be a stay-at-home mom and do what I loved doing best--caring for babies.

Twenty-three months later, David was born in less than a two-hour labor and literally popped into the world on Friday, the 13th. Shock was the best description of the reaction that the doctors and we had for his arrival. George was my blond toe-head and here comes our second son with bright, very bright, orange, red hair. And lots of it! Neither Wes nor I knew of any redheads in our families, but here he was. We looked at each other like the delivery doctor had just told us he was striped and finally someone broke the silence with "it's a boy"! He was so gorgeous. Plump and lively like his brother, it appeared that we had just witnessed another miracle. Not to be!

Two days after David's birth, the Pediatrician arrived to tell us some disturbing news. It seemed that David had a VSD, ventricular septal defect, and it could be dire. The good news was that you could hear a "whoosh" when you put your head on his chest. That meant it was a tiny hole in his heart which created a lot of pressure pushing blood through the opening and making a louder noise than a more massive hole would produce. The bad news was that it could still be fatal or cause for surgery if it did not close on its own. David would need constant monitoring for six weeks and a weekly visit to the Pediatrician before he would be out of the woods. The next six weeks were pure hell in the Simpson's home. Wes and I took turns sitting by David's crib. We had set up an electric monitor so we could hear him turn over, cry, or cough. Neither of us could rely entirely on this little box to care for our infant son, so we were in his room almost every hour throughout the night and day. We were terrified that we would lose him. I could not eat or sleep during this time and could not talk to anyone about how scared I really felt. Wes and I were not even talking to each other.

Spirituality was not discussed, and religion had ceased to be a part of my life. That too can and did change. During this emotionally and physically challenging time with David, I turned to my "God" with a constant prayer that my red-headed baby would survive. Wes tried to be supportive, but our marriage was being tested in the middle of potential tragedy. Many couples divorce during times of adversity, but finally, with nowhere else to turn, we started leaning on each other for strength. I began to rely heavily on Wes for physical and mental strength and Wes looked to me to carry on with as much courage as I could muster. The tragedy became a crisis; the crisis became a situation; and finally, the small hole closed by itself. David began playing on the floor with his brother George. The spiritual journey would continue and lead me to a renewed faith which would eventually save not only my son's life but my life. Faith has been defined as believing in what cannot be seen. I knew every time I looked at David that there indeed was a higher power, an almighty, loving God who loved my son.

Wes was on his own spiritual journey and continued to nurture and teach his two sons. There was no doubt who the father was of these two boys. The physical resemblance was noticeable from birth.

Fathers were still a hot topic in my world, and I continued to write letters to my real father. We still had not met, but he continued to write, and I kept every letter in the special red notebook. One day, this red binder would be exceedingly handy and valuable to its holder. After congratulating me on the birth of our first son, my father moved to New York, and our correspondence continued.

After Law School, we also made a big move from Amish Pennsylvania to a beach resort in Virginia, the place where I was born and spent the first 14 years of my life. Moving to a new city and a new job was extremely exciting for our young family. My trust fund made it possible to buy a beautiful house in an older neighborhood of Rehoboth Beach. Wes opened his own law firm with a partner and funding from my mother's current boyfriend. Family money can create significant problems, and it was the beginning of the end. Apparently, there was just not as much money as had been anticipated, and our budget was being stretched. Since I never had had to worry about finances, we lived in a fairytale world where money was not an issue… until that first summer in Rehoboth Beach. Then the shit hit the fan. There were debts and many expenses. What happened? Quite simply, the trust fund dried up! It was time for me to think about earning an income and joining the workforce. I had never really worked outside the home, except babysitting and a brief stint of taking care of kids in a daycare facility in Switzerland. I did not know where to begin and put it off as long as I could. Afterall, I loved being a stay-at-home mom, and a job search was not part of the plan. For the first time in my adulthood, life was good! I had friendly neighbors, new friends, two beautiful baby boys, a big-shot attorney for a husband, and I was in excellent health. I nursed both my boys until they were over a year old and banned alcohol or drugs of any kind from my diet so that nothing wrong would be passed on to my babies.

We were especially close to a British family that lived across the street. We would join them on their weekend adventures. In exchange with our military surveillance department, Paul was a true Englishman. He had six children, an attractive, supportive wife, and two years to experience as much of the United States as he could. That meant weekend trips to historical sites, like Williamsburg, weekly jaunts to the beach, and lots of time in our backyard pool. Wes was spending more and more time at his Law Firm, and I was busy enjoying my boys every day in every way.

Our home was immaculate: a brick ranch home with a big stone fireplace in the library and a gorgeous lot with huge pecan trees and live oaks. There were many neighborhood cookouts and three months every summer that were spent around our pool. Who knew that all of this would come crumbling down stone by stone?

The second spring in Rehoboth Beach, I decided to take the boys and go visit my mother, who had moved to Calpe, Spain. My grandma Lee was there, which made the trip very exciting. Not only was it an opportunity to show off my two boys, George and David, but I could enjoy the company of my very favorite person, my grandma.

It was exactly two days after my arrival in Spain that I came down with the flu, or so I thought. It was my grandma that posed the question: "Could you be pregnant?" A visit to the local medical center confirmed her suspicion, and there would be a new baby just after Christmas. Wes did not take the news with as much enthusiasm as I had anticipated. We had avoided having financial discussions, and I had not made any attempts to enter the real world of work.

Our daughter, Kate, was born right after the holidays and she almost entered our world in the hospital elevator. It was awfully close, but Wes made it to the hospital in time to see our second bright redhead be born. She was healthy, energetic, and red curls were on top of her perfect-sized head. Did I say she was a girl? I never knew how much I wanted a daughter until I saw her for the first time. The boys became her protectors from the beginning, and we taught her to swim before she could walk. When I was pregnant with Kate, I took the real estate course. It was the only pregnancy that I had to munch on saltine crackers for the first three months, and my fellow students seemed to pick up on my symptoms. I took the licensing exam feeling quite nauseated, but I passed and joined a large firm in town to begin my new career. My mother was the instigator of this new line of work. Over the years, I have not known whether to blame her, salute her, thank her, or condemn her for pushing me into real estate. You can decide.

I did exceedingly well in my first job as a real estate agent and excelled way beyond anyone's expectations, especially mine. I was getting ahead of myself.

* * *

I want to discuss fathers at this point and evaluate Wes as the father of our three children under the age of five. This is easy.

He was devoted to the kids, loved them unconditionally, and tried, really tried, to give them as much attention as possible. It was the balancing act that did us both in. Launching a new law firm and being the best lawyer that he could be took an inordinate amount of time. We hired an English nanny to take care of the kids. We did not want her to be their parent, just their caretaker. Isabel moved in with us and helped tremendously with the childcare, the housekeeping, the cooking, the lifeguarding, and the chauffeuring. Wes and I, unknowingly, began competing for more time to spend at work. We did not realize what was happening and there was no intention to hurt each other or the children. We did. We damaged each other and our family in a way that could not be salvaged or repaired.

* * *

About this time the Admiral and I started communicating again. There had been a few letters, but in 1981, not only did I start saving his messages to that red book, I began keeping my responses. We still had not met, and there always seemed to be a good excuse.

October 1981

"Dear Janet… I loved your letter. I am amazed at what you have done. I want to see you as soon as possible just as you do…. I am off to California this coming week for a business and a lecture at the California Institute of Technology and I am not really ready or knowledgeable enough to give it. Anyway, to get back to our meeting. I don't want just a luncheon meeting either and I want to be alone with you. I believe as you do that the best thing for me to do is to come to Rehoboth and spend the weekend with you. My only problem at the moment is the time for I am quite involved up until the middle of December…. Please be sure I won't let it die this time and we will be together, and I hope it will be soon. Yours, Matt"

December 1981

"Dear Matt… I return from Spain January 2 and now I just have to meet with you…. I am very confused about my feelings for you right now.... In my last letter, I did a lot of bragging about myself, my career, and my family. This letter I just do not feel like bragging. Feelings are a funny thing. You are in touch one minute and confused the next.... In any case, bringing you back into my life has not been easy. I love you, and that is not simple. I love the idea of you—the idea of having a father. God, I spend most of my life quietly and secretly crying out for someone to love me, really love me—just for me—like only a parent can love. And somewhere out there is a father that I have really never met. If that sounds melodramatic, I do apologize.... This thing with you and I is something left hanging and it goes against my entire personality to leave something undone. In fact, it drives me crazy or just to drink and forget it. There does not seem to be any gray area in my life. Everything is black or white. I am always right in there living life to its fullest or I escape and get out. The escape part is the scary part. It is irresponsible, selfish, dangerous, and bound to hurt the people I love.... There are days on end where I do not have a drink. Then—presto—it's release time and I drink six, not two, or smoke a little grass or whatever.... I don't expect miracles. You have your own life and I am not part of it. I cannot say that that does not make me unhappy. It does.... I have decided that I need to know you. Write to me when you can.... I definitely have a void in my life, and I guess that is what I am trying to say. Please do put everything aside early in January so that I can see you.... I cannot wait until we get together and yet I am scared to death.... I am expecting too much.... Let me hear from you and here's to seeing you in 1982. Thirteen is my lucky number and it was thirteen years ago that I discovered you exist. Love, Janet"

December 20, 1981

"My dearest... I loved your letter and you can call me anytime. Your mother always knew me as the Admiral so I guess that is fine.... Never doubt however that I love your mother and am sure if I saw her again the same old chemistry would be there for me. I guess it will always be that way until I die.... You sound like a fascinating person with probably your mother's brains and my bad faults. Please give her my love and have a Merry Christmas, and here is to New Year's. Love, the Admiral"

* * *

Our children were always safe, but we ignored the signals that we were neglecting our parental roles. Wes loved his children, and no one would dispute that, but when the children were young, he made a significant decision to back off being their father. Our world was collapsing. Through all the letters that I had received from my father, the Admiral, I knew that he had also chosen career over family. More specifically, he chose the Navy over his daughter, me. We had regressed from "Love, Daddy" to "Love, Matt" to "Love, the Admiral" in his letters, and I became more distant with the name change.

In my perfect, happy family I was not an innocent bystander. I now had an office, a boss, coworkers, goals, clients, commissions, financial security, and a competitive drive that my company was happy to support. Two lives were created. I was Mommie three nights a week and half of the weekends, and I was the real estate agent 24/7, even when I was with the children. Do I have regrets? You bet. I did not miss many soccer games, birthday parties, or sleepovers, but I did miss what counts—quality time with each of my children. It hurt to continually be making choices between my family and my work. Wes and I were drifting apart in a sea of chaos, passing in the driveway and using phone check-ins as an intimate contact.

Looking back, it was easy to see that we were in an incredibly competitive race to succeed and make lots of money (that was our measure of success). It was easy to throw blame at each other and glaze one of the children in the act. Needless to say, our marriage ended unpleasantly.

*　*　*

At the end of my first year in real estate, I was named the top agent in a 400-member firm. We moved the family three times because of the good "deals." We went through three nannies and early preschools. I took night courses to become a real estate broker and manager. Once you were number one, it was hard to settle for less. I fought to be at the top of the heap and collected many awards, accolades, and much money along the way. The price was the gift that keeps on giving—guilt.

*　*　*

Weaning my daughter before she was a year old was the most painful and upsetting act of motherhood that I had ever encountered. It hurt right down to my bones, and I am talking about physical pain, not just tremendous emotional distress. I had nursed both the boys through their infancy and intended to do the same with Kate. I tried pumping and leaving milk for the nanny, but it didn't work. I was only able to nurse her for seven months. My choices were a mistake. Mothers everywhere are torn apart having to choose between career and family. I really believed that I was different and could do both well.

It had been five years since I smoked dope, drank alcoholically, or put anything up my nose. As soon as I quit nursing Kate, it was back to the races. I had chosen the perfect career for an alcoholic. I believed with all my heart that I could not be one. Almost every day you could find a new construction site opening that had an open bar that began at 4 pm and closed at 8 pm. There goes dinner with the family. Liquid lunches were every day because you had to solicit your clients. Office parties were scheduled at least once a month and booze flowed readily. I am not implying that all real estate agents are drunks because that is not the case. On the contrary, most agents are honest, diligent, family-oriented persons that you would be glad to call your friend. I was not attracted to that individual. I sought out the most competitive, fun-loving, single party goers that I could find. Why? What about my family, my husband, and my three beautiful children? My priorities were upside down.

***

Let's get back on track in the order of events. I still had not met my biological father. Turning thirty was an eye-opener for me. I was the youngest managing broker of the firm and ran the top-producing office of the entire area. My agents decided to have a surprise birthday party for me at the office. Even the top brass stopped by and everyone was in a festive mood. My secretary, Ellen, came up to me and right in my face (I guess she was whispering), said, "You are so lucky. You have a successful lawyer husband, three beautiful children, a huge house on the water, three cars, a boat, and this incredible job. Wow!" I did not respond. I just stared at her like a deer in a car's headlights.

There was only one thought in my head. All I wanted to do was kill myself. *What was wrong with me?*

June 11, 1982

"Dear Admiral… You are either the procrastinator of a lifetime; have been seriously ill; or have decided to write me off permanently. You do underestimate my tenacity.…Maybe you are not aware that I drove to your house in February to see you, left a note, saw your home, toured around the neighborhood—neat town—but unfortunately, missed you. It actually was a turning point in my life. When you hit bottom, no one is going to be there to pull you up but yourself. I was running to the last hope that I thought that I had—you—and ironically, you were not there but in Florida.… No one will know the pain or the joy that my weekend drive to your home caused.… The next move was yours. Call me, plan a visit, or tell me when you will be home so that I can visit. Do not worry about your notoriety or your family; I am and will always be anonymous, a friend of the family, or whatever.… Janet"

I made a promise that I could not keep.

* * *

Making a decision once again to visit my father after the failed attempt to his home was another impulsive move with little forethought and less planning. My only friends were my secretary, several of my top-producing agents, a couple of fellow managing brokers, and my supervisor. These were my party buddies, my drinking friends, and my drug connections. So, I decided to take Rose, my friend/office secretary, and drive to D.C. for two days to meet my father. We left Friday afternoon and drove four hours on route 95, one of

Virginia's busiest interstates to the nation's capital, Washington D.C. You could cut the tension in the car with a knife. I was stressed out and no one was talking. I felt like I was driving to a funeral, not a reunion. Usually I am not at a loss for words, but there was an eerie silence in that Buick.

We arrived at the Omni hotel in Alexandria, right outside the beltway that circles D.C. Two days before, I had telephoned my father and told him I wanted to meet. Actually, that call was a threat. If he did not want to meet me, I would be forced to go back to his home up north and surprise his wonderful family, including his wife. He believed me. I had resorted to blackmail. We arranged to meet in a restaurant in downtown D.C. on the following Saturday. He said that he had business there and that would work out. In other words, it was not a special trip just to see me. The wheels started spinning, however, and I imagined the scene of outstretched arms embracing me with the love of the world in his slate-blue eyes. Would I even recognize him? Or would he be able to pick me out of the busy lunch crowd?

Rose and I were staying at an Omni which had a great tavern, and it was open twenty-four hours a day. After checking in, I headed for the bar and drank my dinner. I was extremely nervous and told Rose that I could not go through with it. After I passed out, morning came, and I had three hours before the grand performance. Fortunately, I had brought some weed with me and went out in the parking lot to calm down. Rose suggested one drink before my infamous lunch, and I thought that was a great idea. We visited the hotel bar one more time. It was soon time for me to be on my way. It was a short ride in lots of traffic, so I took a taxi. At last, I was going to be able to ask, "Are you my father?" and get the answer that I wanted.

Arriving early at the rendezvous spot, I ordered a gin and tonic and watched everybody coming into the restaurant. I do not know how long I waited, but this older man in a dark suit walked up to the booth. Slowly and with a robotic gesture, I stood and extended my hand. He held out both arms and gave me an embrace that would be etched in my memory forever. I did not expect affection and was once again surprised but not shocked.

I felt like I wanted to throw up and was confused by that gesture. The stranger introduced himself as Matt and took a seat across from me. I felt like my hair was standing on end as I tried to gain control of my anxiety. At that moment, I knew that I wasn't breathing normally. How was I going to speak if air was not even coming out of my mouth? I had rehearsed this moment for sixteen years, and I could not remember one of my practiced lines. Did we look alike? This man was not a corpse, and he did not die in a plane crash. Why had my mother mixed up the pieces of the puzzle so much?

***

The Admiral asked if we should order. The running movie in my head did not follow this script. The conversation was driven by his questions about my children, my soon-to-be ex-husband, my job, and what was I doing in D.C. I said very bravely, "I am here to meet you, my father, and thank you for all the letters over the years." I was high, and I was drunk. It was embarrassing, and I just hoped that he did not know how drug-affected I really was. Lunch ended, and I do not remember what was said at the very end. I do recall him looking at his watch, and I did wonder if I was just another appointment. Before he left, he did ask about my mother, and I gave him a full report. That was it.

June 22, 1982

"Dear Janet... I had such a delightful time with you, I just wanted to tell you so. You are a lovely person in addition to being a lovely woman.... I am sure you can do anything you want. Please remember, learn as much as you can for as I said it certainly will open wider the spectrum of any options in the future for you. Love, Matt"

I guess that I performed well at our lunch meeting in Washington, D.C. and was still a highly functioning "problem drinker."

* * *

I do not know exactly when I figured this out, but it was evident to me that I was extremely depressed, disappointed with both my parents and full of guilt and shame about my own family. I tried to stop drinking and just ended up smoking more pot. Maybe I did have a drug problem. I went back to alcohol and did not even try to hide my drinking or drug use. I was entirely out of control.

During this time there was a specialized training for real estate brokers in Charlottesville, Virginia. Every managing broker in the firm was required to attend. We were standing in line for a dinner reservation, and several of us were secretly smoking weed while we waited. I started hitting on one of my cohorts, and he reciprocated by suggesting we go back to his RV and skip the dinner. I share this story because it clearly illustrates just how careless, clueless, and critical my drug and alcohol use had become. It never crossed my mind that wearing his sweater over last night's dress to attend class the next morning was unacceptable or that I should have been mortified. Things were spiraling down fast.

I had been so careless that I was afraid that I might be pregnant. After a scheduled appointment with a gynecologist, it was decided that I needed to plan a hysterectomy. Apparently, I had a fibroid tumor and would abort a fetus if I was pregnant. I did not know what I was doing or what to do. After the surgery, my self-loathing escalated, and I started lying to cover up the lies. In fact, I could not remember what lie I had told to cover up the last lie. The critical business meetings were being ignored. Wes had moved out, and I quit making mortgage payments or paying any bills. The financial structure was beginning to crash.

One night I went drinking at a bar downtown with some coworkers and passed out on Long Island Ice Teas. I woke up in a strange apartment with a nice, good-looking man helping me take a bath in Epsom salts. He was very handsome and did not want sex with me. He told me that I was in trouble and had to stop drinking and drugging. I still do not know who that angel was, but he helped me get home. I had lost my car and had no idea where I might have left it. Later in the day, my boss called to fire me. He apologized for doing it over the phone, but since I rarely went to my office anymore, it was the only way he could let me go. His final words were "Get some help!"

* * *

I had already met my father, so what was the problem? It felt like I had checked off a box on my bucket list and yet I was so disappointed. I had really botched my first encounter with my father and wanted to apologize. I did not know how. A couple of years down the road, I would have the opportunity to not only see the Admiral again but to forge a lasting relationship until his death.

Chapter 5: Learning to Fly Straight

Since locating and meeting my father did not solve my problems, I still was not sure what was wrong with me. There was good news. I was willing to get help and checked into a psychiatric hospital to fix what was broken. My children were ages five, seven, and nine, and their mother was missing, physically and emotionally. I asked my friend who was driving me to the loony bin to make a pit stop to pick up a six-pack of beer for the twenty-minute ride to the hospital. She agreed. I still did not see alcohol as a problem. I just needed to rest, to cool off, to ground myself, to feel safe, and get people off my back. All the issues were apparently caused by other people. I had a long list to blame, starting with my mother and my father. It had been a long time since I had slept (days or weeks), so maybe I could get some sleep. What I expected in this hospital did not happen. The first day I was introduced to a substance abuse counselor who tried to give me a book called the *Big Book*. I told her that I didn't need any such book, as I could quit drinking anytime that I wanted to stop—as long as I was locked up, that is. I was assigned a roommate that liked to talk to the goldfish in the tank by the front door. She became my new cocaine dealer when she was released. Being extremely restless, I was permitted to go to the gym and play tennis against the back wall anytime that I wanted to. I still did not sleep and spent the first few nights hitting tennis balls… 1 am, 2 am, 3 am, and so on. The fourth day I decided this was all a big mistake and I decided to break out of the facility. I scaled a fourteen-foot anchor fence behind the outdoor tennis court and jumped to freedom. The first car that looked inviting was a Volkswagen full of adolescents who were visiting a friend. I had one credit card and a list of what I wanted to do upon my escape. The teens thought this was great fun and took me downtown on the street where the bars were located. I found a booth, ordered a German beer and began completing my "to do" list. Today, people call this a bucket list or putting your ducks in a row. I borrowed a phone and called a male friend to bring me some weed or cocaine and have some sex. He obliged on all counts, and there was only one thing left on my list. I wanted to kill myself and had to figure out how. I left the hotel and started walking. About eighteen miles was how far I walked and was picked up by a Ford truck on a road that runs through a state park. He was my second guardian angel and took charge of the situation. He asked me a simple question, "Where do you want me to take you?" I had no idea and no answer. I told him my psychiatric hospital plight and that I just needed to get away. He gave me two choices: "Call the police or call your psychiatrist." I really had to think about it. I called the hospital, and they sent a taxi to pick me up. My Chinese psychiatrist was waiting at the hospital and gave me a shot of something to get me to sleep. The next morning the doc showed up and took me outside the hospital grounds for a walk. He pointed out that he was wearing tennis shoes and could outrun me. His next words meant nothing at the time, but they did change my life forever: "You are bipolar. It is a brain disorder with no cure. It is sometimes called manic/depression, and there is a treatment." I asked very few questions and inwardly denied everything he said. We went back to the ward, and I stayed in the hospital another four weeks without any incident. However, I did have alcohol withdrawal and shook for at least two of those long weeks.

* * *

I was thirty-two, unemployed, had not eaten properly for months, and weighed less than a hundred pounds. I had passed skinny and gone right to anorexic. My husband had taken custody of our children and was ready to discuss his full custody. What a nightmare! Amidst all this drama, my mother flew into town to save the day. I do love my mother, but there have been periods that I really did not like her, and this was one of those times. She believed if we took a trip to the Outer Banks in North Carolina with the kids, I would be able to "shake" whatever was bothering me. Those were her words. I do not know what she and the children did down in Nags Head, but I found a bar and got drunk. I told her it was only beer and not hard liquor, so I was OK.

* * *

My older brother, Edward, whom I had not seen for years, was remarried and living on an island in the Caribbean. Our mother had told him about my situation. He called and offered to pay my rent on a new townhome so I would have a place to live with the children when they were not with Wes. It was a very generous offer, and I would have turned it down if I had any other options. I had not learned to swallow my pride and ask for help when I needed it. There was one significant condition: "Stay away from drugs and alcohol and get treatment for the bipolar disorder." Hitting bottom is a term you hear in Alcoholic Anonymous meetings. I thought that I had already hit bottom, but I kept bouncing off the bottom. I had tried AA and NA. I could admit that I was an addict and an alcoholic but was not willing to accept what that meant. Abstinence is a powerful word. Getting sober was the most challenging task that I had ever attempted. I migrated around the meetings for three years and could not get my act together. In other words, I kept going back to alcohol and drugs. During this self-absorbed period of my life, I began my "Walk to Nowhere."

The temperature had dropped and there was some daylight, but I did see the beginning of sunset over the ocean. Parking my car in the deserted public parking spot in Sandbridge, I really did not know what I was doing. Sitting in the car was painstaking, as my anxiety level was higher than the seagulls I was watching. I needed to move.

Why didn't I bring a jacket, a hoodie, a sweatshirt? As I approached the surf, I was also aware of a strong wind and the sand flying into my feet and shins. It was too bad that none of those natural phenomena influenced my decision to take a walk, a long walk. About fifty yards along the shore's edge, viewing the raging waves at sea, I also realized that I was extremely angry. Cussing at the ocean, I was trying to understand why I was so furious and whom or what I was blaming this time. I was angry at God. To that point in time, my belief in a heavenly father was very murky. Yet here I was yelling at something or someone that I could not see. *Why am I cursing at a bunch of waves rolling onto the beach?* Maybe if I kept walking, I could find the answers. As darkness advanced, so did I, but I had no destination.

My blond hair, which was past my shoulders, was blowing in hundred different directions. Walking barefoot in the wet sand was no longer bearable so I moved higher on the shore to continue my journey to wherever I was going. Surely I would find solace or at least become less agitated as I progressed. I was very cold. However, my brain was on overdrive and I had what can only be called an epiphany. *I do believe in God, because I am yelling at someone. Keep walking, Janet! Maybe more answers will come to you.*

I not only left my shoes in the car, but all sense of rational thinking. It was not safe to walk the beach alone and hypothermia was a definite possibility. I don't remember how far I had gone before I knew that I needed some shelter. It was getting colder and the wind was whipping up dried seaweed and anything else it could find to throw into my path. The beach was completely deserted, so I headed over the dunes to a line of beach bungalows on stilts. I selected the one cloaked in darkness and failed to find an open shed or porch where I might find refuge. However, I discovered an outside shower with a deflated raft hanging on a shower hook. This would have to do. Time was passing, but I had no way to know where I was or if it was midnight or time for sunset. I covered my body with the raft and cowered in a corner of the bath house. There was no door, and you can imagine my surprise when company arrived. A black Labrador invited himself in and proceeded to lie next to me and keep me warm. I don't know how long we cuddled together, but it was getting lighter and I must have fallen asleep. I needed to vacate my overnight home and continue my walk to nowhere. The black Labrador decided to accompany me to the beach and walk along the water's edge with me for what seemed a long, long way. Eventually, he turned around and headed back toward the bungalows. He was a saint and maybe a sign from this new God that I was trying to get to know.

My journey continued along the beach until I saw more houses, a small store, and a few jeeps parked over the dunes. I can only imagine what I looked like after walking thirty miles to Duck, North Carolina. I had no money, no ID, and my legs felt like they had been run over by a truck. My calf muscles were cramping, and it was difficult to walk one more step. A fellow in a pickup drove to where I was standing and asked if he could give me a ride to somewhere. Another knight in shining armor. I suggested that he drive me to Nags Head and leave me at Shoney's. This was another divine intervention, as I knew there was an AA breakfast meeting at 9 am at the restaurant, and that is where I needed to be.

The series of events that took place that morning at the Outer Banks were quite amazing and somewhat unbelievable. I thanked my unknown chauffeur and proceeded into Shoney's. I knew that my personal appearance was shocking and it was time for true humility to approach this AA group. There were two tables pushed together and a fellow got another chair for me and said, "Welcome. You can sit here with us." It was the first time in a very long time that I felt like I was a part of "us." One woman handed me a brush and another older woman said, "What do you want for breakfast? It's on me."

I do not remember anyone's name at that meeting, nor what was discussed. After the meeting closed, one gentleman asked me if he could buy me some shoes, flip-flops. He had another agenda. Once we were in his truck, he asked very kindly if he could give me a ride to Helen's. I did not respond immediately because I was thinking, *who the hell is Helen?* He explained that she was a dedicated member of AA with thirty-four years of sobriety who helped newcomers and lived two miles away. I was shocked when I was told that she was expecting me.

I do not remember much about my time with Helen except that she was old, from New York, spoke very directly, and did not mince words about how screwed up I was and what I needed to do about that. Another coincidence had to do with a woman's AA retreat going on further down the coast in Okacroke. She told me she was going to take me to that group of women, and I was to find another fellow New Yorker, named Linda, and ask her to be my AA sponsor. I could hardly walk, as my legs felt like Jell-O, but I knew that there was no doubt about me following Helen's direction. I was not sure what that meant, but as they say, the rest is history. After locating Linda, I asked for help and she agreed to be my sponsor.

This story does not have a happy ending. My pride, my addictions, and my lack of humility needed a whole lot of work. Back at Rehoboth Beach, I did start going back to AA meetings, spoke to my new sponsor daily, and began taking my medications as prescribed. However, there was still one big problem. I wanted someone to fix me, forgive me, love me, and take responsibility for me. A father? Is that really what was missing?

* * *

Years later, I was going to answer my own question. Accepting life on life's terms is a daunting proposition. Accepting the family you are given is how you learn to love and not blame or judge. I located my biological father and that was a gift. He was really never missing. He was and is a part of me. His genes are in my genes. I am who I am, in part, because of who my father is and who my mother is. It is time for me to be who I am and accept the bad, the ugly, and the good. It is time to not only leave the nest and fly, but to fly straight. Learning to love myself and accept who I am becoming is a tall order. I need to learn how to be my own best parent. It will take years of therapy, counseling, and recovery. It is time for me to take responsibility for my own actions and change my life.

* * *

There was a great deal of repair work to be done. Over the years I have had many surgeries to repair a bad back, a dysfunctional shoulder, an arthritic knee, a deteriorating neck, and more. However, this was the first time that I experienced an emotional bankruptcy that surgery would not fix. I needed help, and I knew where to get it. My third rehab gave me answers that I had not heard before. "Stop drinking the first drink and do it one day at a time. Stop using the first drug and do that one day at a time. Go to as many AA or NA meetings as possible with a minimum of ninety meetings in ninety days. Get a sponsor and work the 12 Steps of the program. Get into service work and help others that are in recovery." This all fits into one neat paragraph, and it is a simple program. My sponsor tells me, "It is a simple solution, and all you have to do is work the program and turn your whole life around."

Recovery included therapy and counseling; I had been dually diagnosed with the bipolar disorder and a substance abuse problem. Lucky me! Gratitude would come later. Both were diseases with no cures but could be treated. The bipolar disorder proved to be severe and medication-resistant in my case. Lithium did not affect my mood swings whatsoever. It would take years to find a medication "cocktail" that would work.

During this time, the letters continued sporadically from the Admiral, and both of us were spending time trying to mend our bodies and souls.

October 25, 1983

"My dear Janet... I hasten to answer your letter which has really made me a very sorry person for all that has happened to you. I have contributed to so much hurt to so many individuals in my life I certainly am not proud of myself. As my life draws to a close, I am particularly sad about it. What will the account balance actually be only the good Lord will know. My only real message to you is yes I do love you, and you are an important person. My actions have certainly not shown much but as my close family will tell you, I am a pretty cold person outside but a mass of contradictions within myself. Yes you are in my heart and I want you to know it for it is never too late in life to actually say things and let the truth out. Your genes are half mine, so you are actually part of me and all the background of my ancestors.... Please don't worry that I have rejected you in my heart. My seventh-sixth birthday is in November and I have to go to the hospital here to be operated on and know anything can happen to one at my age and so want to get this message to you now.... I was delighted about your going back to school. Please don't give up. It has never been in my nature to do that and I am sure it isn't in yours deep down.... The slogan "Press On" has solved and will always solve the problems of the human race.... People will tell you I was always an assured man. During the war I would be so frightened I would want to throw up. Everyone would think I had no feelings on the subject as I went on my way. How little they knew! Anyway be of stout heart and remember I do love you even though the circumstances have not been where I could do much about it. Love, Matt"

This letter stopped me in my tracks. It was written on my father's stationery which identified him as an Admiral at the top of the page. It was an apology and an admission of hurt in the life of an extremely successful, accomplished man, my father. I was so proud and humbled by the message that he sent. I was also apprehensive about his health and quit focusing exclusively on mine. I had become so self-centered in the extreme that I forgot about my parent as a human being doing the best he can at the time. Our relationship shifted, and overnight it became healthier than it had been ever. The next letter sounded more fatherly and gave me the support and encouragement that I needed during this challenging time.

December 3, 1984

"Dear Janet… Just a line to let you know I am home and all went as well as anything goes in the hospital.… Hope this finds you in good spirits and that all is not lost.… There is one thing I can say about old age and that is fortunately you only have to do it once. So enjoy your youth and take care of yourself. If one does doesn't have their health they have nothing.… It is the richest possession we ever have in our life. Love, Matt"

July 5, 1985

"Dear Admiral… It is strange that when I write to you, I never know if you will receive the letter, if you are alive or dead.… I always hope that you are alive and do read my letters. While the letters might be sent with long intervals between them, you never are out of my thoughts and my feelings. Every Father's Day, sad days, every self-evaluation day, even happy days—I think of you.

I have found another father since I wrote to you last. I finally found out about a higher power, someone or something so much more powerful and loving than anyone or anything I have ever known. God seems like a good title.… I am not talking about religion, but I am talking about a spiritual experience that has made a big difference in my life. There have been too many coincidences to call coincidences anymore. When I give up, when I surrender—there really is someone else running this world and my life. I am a miracle. I should not be alive and yet continue to "press on".… I do not even know you and I love you with all my heart. I cannot explain that, and it just makes me cry to write about it. That is not explainable either because emotion is something that I have learned to stuff and I very rarely cry. I think that I have been bleeding emotionally for a very long time and only the passage of time will take care of those old hurts and pains.

In your last letter you mentioned that if one doesn't have their health, they have nothing. I do agree and have been working very hard during the past few months to regain mine. I am sorry, so sorry, for what I have done in the past few years to those I love by not taking care of me. I spent six weeks in March in a drug and alcohol rehabilitation hospital after completely losing control over drugs. Not only did I hit a new bottom but I hit insanity and now am fighting for my life. That fight also includes the final stages of a divorce that I never wanted and a child custody suit over three beautiful children that are my life. I am still trying to finish school and am only able to hold my head above water financially because of mother's generosity. None of the material things mean anything. Every day, I just want to be loved for who I am and have the blessing of loving others. I still love my husband and this divorce is complicated. It sounds so clichéd, but I am having trouble imagining a life without him, and failing to provide a father for my children has devastated me. I know firsthand how important that one is. I guess this letter is also written out of fear that it will be the last opportunity that I have to write to you. As I said earlier, I feel that way on every letter, but this time I just feel uneasy. If there were any way that I could see you again in your lifetime, I would like that to happen. I will fly to wherever or meet you wherever you said if that was possible. I need to see you again in this new life which is more a part of reality. Am being forced to grow up, to accept responsibility for what is, and to accept what isn't. If there is any way that I can see you in person, please call me and let me know.... Admiral, I would never cause you any trouble with your family and do not want anything from you other than your presence. If your health does not allow travel, I will fly up north, to Florida or wherever. If it is not possible to ever see you again, than this letter will have to carry a big message.

I am sorry that I did not encourage or actively seek a relationship with you after I found out the truth about you being my father. I was too self-centered, too selfish, and too caught up in the material things of this world. I had to lose all those things in order to understand what was really important. I am sorry that I never gave you the opportunity to be proud of me, like I am proud of you.

I am sorry that I only seemed to write or contact you when I was in need rather than looking at your needs and wants. That is the same way that I have called on God all my life. When things were hopeless, I got on my knees and asked for help.

Now, every night I thank God for another day of living and ask him for strength to "press on." You see—I finally learned that I cannot do it alone and since I am human and not perfect, I make lots of mistakes. I have also accepted the fact that I was a mistake from the moment that I was born. But that's OK because good things do come out of bad things sometimes.

I hope this letter does find you alive and healthy. More important, I hope it finds you happy, and you can just smile a little knowing that someone down here in Virginia loves you very much. People keep telling me that I am a survivor and I am trying to not only believe them but to show them. I am also trying to get to know who Janet really is and I suppose that is a big reason for writing to you. You are a big part of who I am which might explain the persistence and determination.

May God watch over you and your family and bring us together again if that be His will. Amen! With love always, Janet"

* * *

The divorce was final, and the custody battle was over. My children were moving 1,500 miles away with their father. It was devastating and happened the same month that I picked up a one-year chip for staying sober, 365 exceptionally long days. This little cheap, plastic token meant the world to me. I did not drink or use and continued to get direction in my life that was healthy and incredible from where I had been.

There were two significant events during that first year of sobriety that would shape my life forever.

I was sober four months and got a call from the owner of a very prestigious real estate firm in the area. He knew my history, all of it, and wanted to talk to me about a job. The offer was managing broker of his top-producing office and a handsome salary to go with it. I had been unemployed for three years and knew there had to be a catch. Indeed, there was a condition. My first sales meeting I was told that I had to disclose to all the agents that I was a recovering alcoholic and addict. At the time it did seem like a huge request. Courage is a funny thing. If I were honest, open, and willing to accept his offer, I did believe that somehow, someway I could do what he required. This would be the first time to admit that I was in recovery to anyone outside of the meetings. That day did come and thank God, I had learned how to ask for help, to pray, and to have faith that things would work out. My AA sponsor was my most prominent cheerleader and gave me the strength to follow through. A second career was launched and would continue for the next seven years.

The second climatic event that occurred in that first year of sobriety was that I met my future husband. My divorce was final, my children lived with their father, and I was not looking for a relationship. I was looking for sex and found it in all the wrong places. There were many one-night stands, and the only thing that I did right was to date only men that were in recovery. Somewhere in the chaos of starting a new job, visiting my kids, chasing the "rabbit," going to meetings, seeing my psychiatrist and counselor, and spending time with my sponsor, I stopped long enough to breathe and literally smell the ocean. The beach was still my place of solace and provided some sense of serenity. Maybe there, I could take a personal inventory and make some rational decisions.

I do not want you to be wondering about the rabbit. His name is Midnight, and he is a fifteen-pound pet that my oldest son left with me when he went to live with his father. Midnight has an incredibly annoying habit of escaping from his hut and taking off around the neighborhood. There are not many rabbits, out and about, so someone usually calls me to report a sighting. I finally found Midnight a home with a friendly veterinarian down the block.

Another decision that I made one night on the beach was to quit sleeping around and to have more respect for who I was becoming. Accept the fact that I might live alone for the rest of my life and be grateful that I was alive, period. Maybe the recovery stuff was working. In any case, I stopped dating and began a regular life, including eating, exercising, and sleeping. The rewards were phenomenal. At the time, I was way too thin, very weak, and really did not have the stamina that my new job required. I was anemic and still trying every medication possible to treat my bipolar disorder. The side effects were expected and unavoidable. One pill produced a feeling of unconsciousness during the middle of the day, and another one caused such paranoia that I was afraid of my own shadow. Weight gain was a likely side effect when I did not want any extra pounds. Lack of sleep was a big problem, and there did not seem to be any prescription that would help me not awake at 1:16, 2:32, or 4:11 am. I hated digital clocks that light up your bedroom with those huge green numbers. Taking care of Janet was a full-time job. About this time, I received an important, encouraging letter from my father. Who am I kidding? Every letter from the Admiral was significant.

July 1985

"My dear Janet... I received your letter and hurry to respond to it. You certainly have gone thru a lot, but I pray that you find the strength and resolve to continue to fight the problems with all your resolve. I am very concerned that you really lick the drug problem whether it is alcohol or the other.... Certainly, we can and will meet again, and I will call you at the number you gave me.... I love to swim and play golf, but for the time they are a no-no. There is only one good thing about getting old, and that is that one only has to do it once! However, I don't feel old and my brain works like a Gatling gun and writes reams of things that I study about and am sure no one will ever really be interested in, but it does help me. My idea of the real tragedy would be not to be able to read or that I didn't have all my "marbles." However, many people tell me the crazy people don't know it, so it really doesn't bother them. I don't want to try it! Please, I beg of you to hang in there and fight your problems. I will pray for you but am not sure the good Lord will listen to me. Love, Matt"

My father's summation on "crazy people" certainly hit home and contributed to my denial of bipolar disease for the next decade. I was learning so much so fast that it was difficult to stay on track and stay sober. Sober people told me: "Just don't drink or use drugs, and things would get better." I just had no idea what to put on my wish list. My sponsor told me not to try as I would incredibly shortchange myself. As always, she was right.

You have undoubtedly heard the axiom that when you are not looking is when you find somebody you want to be with. Well, it happened. I was sitting in this crowded fellowship hall before a meeting, and this guy walks in with a blue kerchief holding his hair off his forehead. He was dressed in all-black leather, his motorcycle garb, and was sitting at the main table about fifteen feet away. He turned his head and looked straight at me. He had the most beautiful, captivating eyes that I had ever seen. *Who is this man?* Wait! I was not supposed to be looking. Fate, *kismet*, the stars being aligned, I do not know, but we made a connection. So much for being celibate. For the next three-and-a-half years, Chris and I spent getting to know each other, forging a friendship, and merging our lives. It was not a walk in the rose garden. There were spats, periods of silence, and finally compromises. We both came to the relationship with lots of baggage which had to be weighed, sorted, exposed, and accepted. It was a tedious journey at times, but our love, our dedication to each other, and our need to be together won over and we have now been married thirty-one years.

* * *

That was an immense jump in time and not fair to this story. Where was the Admiral in all this? Most of my letters to my father were long venting epistles that were an attempt to explain my past, understand the present, and predict my future. I did receive some pearls of wisdom in the responses from Matt.

October 1985

"Dear Admiral... Some days I am happy; I laugh; I cry; I feel good; I feel grateful to be alive. Using drugs and alcohol for the past twenty years, somewhere along the line, feelings left and numbness set in. In fact, I have been a robot for the past couple years. It feels wonderful to be human again.... I was such an overachiever, was so busy trying to get approval from everybody, and fighting so long to be the best so others would accept me—that I thought perfect was the only acceptable goal. I was fixed on perfectionism. Needless to say, I always fell short and as a result, hated myself for failing. At thirty-four, I finally found out that less than perfect is not only OK, but that it is human.... Just because someone does not love me, that does not mean that I am unlovable.... My biggest miracle is my three children. They love and accept me for who I am despite the hell they have been through.... Today, I have developed trust in other people, and that has given me friends. Friends are a totally new concept for me, and I now know what I have been missing in a friend.... I have goals that are really very simple—to have serenity, peace of mind, acceptance, or whatever you want to call it, and to be the best that I can in this life. Someone gave me a plaque which states: 'Your life is a gift from God, and what you do with that life is your gift to God.' I like that, and I believe it. Love, Janet"

October 4, 1985

"Dear Janet... Years ago I watched a television program with Lillian Roth. She wrote, 'I will cry tomorrow,' which was her life. It really opened my eyes to the problems one faces with either dope or alcohol. She told me only she could solve the problem. Love of husband or family meant nothing and until the day arrived that she made up her mind to do it, nothing was going to change her life. She said she had to go thru the whole routine all the way to the gutter before she made her mind up to do something. She took charge.... As to my health, I have bounced back much to my delight. I even play golf again, even if I am terrible now.... I am working again in my technical consulting and using my IBM computer like crazy. We go to London this Wednesday where I will do business with some of my former friends from Africa and the Middle East and then on down to Rome where I will lecture on carbon fourteen dating and its use in historical research and what I did years ago on St. Tom's tomb for Pius the 12th.... Please tell your Mother that she should not think it was a mistake and I hope she doesn't think that has been the problem. I just hope you will find out that you are a person and nothing was a mistake and the only thing you have to do is to make sure you, yourself are in control of your own fate. It all depends on you, not your mother, nor me, or anybody else but yourself. I know you can do what you set out to do.... You are a person and a good one and should not have all the insecurity or complex that you seem to have.... Life is no song and dance and I can attest to that, but no one said it was supposed to be a bed of roses.... I am glad that my wife stood by me and that we are still together after all these years. It wasn't easy for her I know for I was a wild young aviator and went to all the wars, and she raised the children most of the time. I studied and worked hard to get where I am, but it wouldn't have happened if she hadn't stood by me. She had every reason to leave me but believed when one is married it is in sickness and trouble until death. We will celebrate our fifty-third wedding anniversary this month. She is really the strength in the family. I guess mothers are like that, and I am sure yours is the same.

At the moment I am engaged in writing a complete story of my life and the problems, defeats, and fun. It isn't for publishing but for the children, and I will see you get a copy for I try to tell it like it is. Naturally, there will be a lot unsaid for I wouldn't cover a lot of things in it. I kept a journal during my years in the Navy for forty-three years and it makes interesting reading now in light of the history that has gone by for I talk about Hitler, Mussolini, and many things over those years as we walked the road to World War II. Then there is the time when I have the Task Force in the Yellow Sea with the run from the Han to the Yalu in the Korean War as the ground support for the 1st Marine Division. Anyway, I will have fun doing it and do like to use my IBM, so you see I am busy and feeling much better. Love, Matt"

February 2, 1986

"Dear Janet… We always seem to be at the other place when we try to get together.…. If you came thru Jacksonville I would go see you but that is not very satisfactory and would rather make it to Rehoboth.… I hope you are really hanging in there on your rebuilding of your life. I know you can do it. I will do my best to help complete part of the puzzle for all of life is really a puzzle and we have only one to live and it will be all over all too soon so make the most of it. Love, Matt"

April 22, 1986

"Dear Matt… I did complete college and will be graduating May 17. I know it is too much to expect you to attend but I will ask anyway. I am a glutton for rejection, but I am working on that too.… Could we meet in D.C.? When? I need to see you. I need to talk to you face to face. The letters help but I know now that I need all the help that I can get in order to survive. Persistence and "press on" have helped tremendously and I guess this is one of those days that putting one foot in front of the other is what that means. I am my worst critic and am finding out that it is OK not to be perfect, to make mistakes, and to suffer that condition known as "humanness." I always have a great deal that I want to say to you but am afraid of saying too much.… I am discovering that life is an adventure. I was very happy to hear that you did write your autobiography and do hope you will give me a copy. I need to tell you that my children know about you and that you are my father. Children are so accepting and not judgmental. I wish that you could meet them. They are the one thing that I did right, and I know that they really are a gift from God. When all the escapes failed and it came time to face reality and discover life on life's terms, the children and I made a pact. No more lies, no more secrets, and we would try to build a life based on trust. It is not happening overnight, but the love is there and through honesty, George, David, and Kate are beginning to trust their mother, ME.... Please take care of yourself and remember that I love you. With love, Janet"

* * *

Part of recovery is the willingness to make amends to anyone that you harmed in your past. Being drunk and high when I first met my father was at the top of that list. The cherry blossoms were still blooming in Washington, D.C. on May 18, 1986. My father was getting older by the week, and my sponsor suggested that I go see him sooner than later. She agreed to go with me, and we set out for our nation's capital. I was about to learn the magic of forgiveness.

Meeting at a different restaurant and having realistic expectations set the stage for me to not say that I was sorry, but to describe the changes in my life and ask for forgiveness for my unacceptable behavior at our initial meeting five years before. We had stayed in touch with the letters, so I did not expect any big surprises. Maybe we would not recognize each other.

May 19, 1986

Dear Matt,"I will have on a blue dress.

Dear Janet, "I have on a blue suit."

I was shocked how old my father had gotten, and he shared with me that he was battling bone cancer. He was skinny, and his suit just hung off his shoulders. My father was still a handsome man, and I knew those piercing blue eyes could see right through me. Anxiety, fear? I remembered all the encouragement and support that I had gotten before this lunch. I had gotten clear advice, to be Honest, Open, and Willing (one of those crucial acronyms, HOW to behave). I hoped it would work.

He gave me a kiss on the cheek and sat across from me facing the bar. I always try to sit facing the front door, and that day was no exception. That position gives me a good feeling of being able to escape, and I feel less claustrophobic in a restaurant. Strange? It is a seating preference that has stayed with me for an exceedingly long time. Just sitting in the right chair gives me more self-confidence and I needed all that I could get. It was time for a little self-talk. *You are OK! This is going to work out. It's OK!* Peace began to settle in, and I started to feel very connected to this man—my father. How could I ever doubt the truth? We were two kindred spirits, a father and a daughter, discovering each other after thirty-five years. A movie? A dream? No, this was the reality. As he spoke, I began to understand why there was acceptance—there was no judgment. His grandfather, his father, and his brother, Dick, were all alcoholics. Dick was in a twelve-step program, and the Admiral quit drinking in his twenties because he knew he had the potential to be an alcoholic. Yes, he did understand this part of me.

I really wanted to remember the moment—I wrote a list of messages and reflections immediately following our lunch, so I would never forget. Perception is very personal, and that is what I thought my father was trying to share with me during our one-on-one conversation.

The Messages
Self-pity = "self-defeating, useless"

Self-awareness = "Discover what the problem is, and you are halfway there."

"Don't look back!" "Don't play what-ifs?"

Defective = "We are all defective in some way."

Learn = "You should never stop. Keep options—all doors open."

I paraphrased the words of wisdom that my father was passing on to his daughter:

"Being illegitimate was not your mistake, it was mine, and mistakes are a part of living. Experiences are mistakes!"

"Each of us has to be responsible for our own lives—you can't blame someone else."

The Admiral shared once again how when he was sixteen and enlisted (by lying about his age), he begged his father to get him out of the Navy and his father said NO.

"Achievements don't measure happiness. My pride was in the success of my children, and you are one of those—my child."

My Reflective Feelings

The pieces are not shattered. The picture is clearer. The puzzle is beginning to take shape and all the pieces fit. I am OK!

I love this man. I am a part of his life and he is a part of mine. We have touched each other just like a butterfly. I felt him land ever so softly on my life, rest for a moment, and gently, but swiftly take flight again.

Pride—what a gift to have this man as my father? He is human but so special. His tragedies have taught him well. Living with any pain is possible for the privilege of living.

"Perseverance—press on." I really heard that the survival instinct is extraordinarily strong.

Touch—I wanted to hold him, to love him. I caressed his cheek as we were leaving and was not afraid.

The prayer from St. Francis was emerging from somewhere, "It is better to love than to be loved." What a gift to have both. His eyes told his story—a life of experiences (some mistakes), seventy-seven years of learning, of process, not perfection.

It upset me, and I was hurt to discover that his wife did not know about me. I was still a secret, not a part, a whole part of his life. I was a "missing piece," and that was OK to be a missing piece all by myself. I wanted more of him, but I was grateful if that was all I got. It was more than I ever imagined. The promises that we read in an AA meeting were coming true.

He made me feel like going forward, like living life to the fullest, giving to others all that I had got and not being afraid to look at the past or shut the door on it. The past was full of my mistakes, but they were my experiences that made the meeting with my biological father, on that day, possible.

Can I accept life on life's terms? He was dying—there might not be any more todays. I did have a daily reprieve, and any gift is precious. That day was the first day of the rest of my life. Receiving an award of a father was something I never expected, and recovery was giving that to me. Sobriety was giving me a father.

Thank you, God. Thank you to all the twelve-step programs. Thank you for my sponsor, Linda. This day could not have been done alone. I do not have to "do life" with a boulder on my back, to meet life and all the realities by myself. My twelve-step program taught me that and gave me people whom God chose to put in my life when I needed them most. That was a gift! These were the thoughts and introspections that followed that significant luncheon in Washington, D.C.

We made plans to meet in Florida the following month so he could meet my oldest son who was then at the University of Florida in Gainesville. The Admiral was headed south to stay in his winter home on the west coast of Florida. I could not wait to call George and plan this rendezvous with a new miracle in my life.

May 26, 1986
"Dear Janet... Just a note to tell you that it was fun to see you and to know all you have done to help yourself. No one else can do it for you and as we said one must live with their decisions.... Today was Memorial Day, and I gave a speech.... Enclosed is something that was written years ago that I unearthed from my files for the talk.
On Christmas day in 1943, I lost one of my crew on the take off for faraway Turk Island and Sector 1. Following are my feelings that far-off day of long ago.
Ask the Winds
We have gone forth like winds: on Lost Bataan,
Deep in New Guinea's jungles, thunder high
Above Australian reefs we rode the dawn
Blanching across the long Pacific sky.
Search for our bones on steaming Burmese coasts
Or seek our smoke plumes on Tibetan snow
Or trace the pattern of our shivering ghosts
Along Attu when Arctic winters blow.
Hearken above North Atlantic's roars
For motors bringing home to friendly lands,
And when you reach the Mediterranean shores
Filter the waves and sift the desert sands.

Kindred who seek us thru the world's wide ends,
Ask of the rain and thunder, ask the winds.
Dawn and the Sunset
Surely they loved the world no less than we
Theirs was the dawn; theirs the sunset, too.
For them, the earth poured out its sweets, the sea
Caught, as for us, the heavens very blue.
They had heard music, known the soft caress
Of woman's (sp) gentle presence. In their eyes
Had carried hopes of home and happiness
And long remembrance. All this wonder dies.
The hills of home, the well-loved fruitful plain
Will vainly wait. They will not come again—
The rain at dusk has cooled the torrid air,
And from blazing stars washed out the dust.
While on some stranged (sp), scorched speck of land, and bare,
A twist of metal settles into rust.
…. I will write more when I get up North. Take care of yourself and hang in there. It is a life-and-death matter. Yours, Matt"

Finally, I had a connection with my father and was learning how to fly straight.

* * *

September 6, 1986
"Dear Admiral… I love my work and I still have a difficult time not being a perfectionist, not being overly competitive about a project, and not trying to bring all my creativity in overnight. The balance is what I am looking for with the career, the children, my relationships, and

of the utmost importance—my AA program. It has been ten months since I have had a drink or drug, and the only way that works is one day at a time.... I still do not have any relationship with anyone in my family and that hurts. In fact, I feel closer to you right now than I do to Mother or my brothers and sister. AA has become my immediate family. I don't know if that is good or bad but today I want to live and that is progress.... You are one of the few people in the world that I can talk to about my feelings and try to be me, even if it is only in letters.... I have been spending a great deal of time analyzing why I am alive today. My record is extremely extraordinary in that several suicide attempts failed that should have succeeded. That is by the grace of God because I did everything in my power to make them successful. Now, I see that they were successful because they failed. Last week, a friend who was back drinking heavily shot himself and was buried. I have lost quite a few friends to drugs, jail, or they just disappear. After I ask the question *why I survived*, I immediately ask *for what purpose?* I know that these are questions men much greater than me have asked for centuries, but like most questions, I am one of those people who have to find the answers themselves. Just that fact has almost killed me, but "thee of little faith" is me. And that will not change overnight. In any case, the only answer that keeps coming back is so simple it hurts. I am here to give love and service to whoever I can and live each day the best that I can.... I do not understand the idea of you have to have something, to give it away.... I do not know if I have anything to give. I seem to love too much, to feel too intensely, to take life too seriously, to sense to extremes, and to seek more than most. These are things that I am afraid to admit to anyone, but they are me. Please be honest and just give me some feedback. Most days I do live each day like it were my last and it makes each day very long, very intense, very important. At the end of the day, I am exhausted.... Love, Janet"

September 20, 1986
"My dear Janet... There is a great deal more to love than taking and I have learned over the years giving is better.... Each day I say, *today is the first day of the rest of my life*, and forget yesterday. You are right about planning and not trying to plan the outcome. Your Coast Guard friend seems like a nice person. I am sure with your background you have a great deal to give to many people in this world besides your children. Love, Matt"

* * *

The letters became more sporadic. The Admiral was having cancer treatments, his wife was battling severe health issues, and my life was centered around recovery, my new relationship, the real estate career, and my children. I made several trips to Colorado to visit my kids and always returned home extremely depressed. They had a stepmother and seemed to be happy in their schools and in their lives. It would be years before I discovered the truth. Had I known what was happening in Colorado, I would have kidnapped my kids and run away where no one could find us. Does that sound dramatic? Looking back still hurts because I probably was not capable of being the mother that they deserved or taking any definitive action at that time. I was still struggling with my own sobriety and trying to remain stable to keep the relationships with my children intact.

Miracles were taking place in all aspects of my life. The real estate office was thriving, and I was promoted to Vice President of the company. One of the fallouts from working in real estate is that you move a lot. Great deals pass your desk, and you are in a new house before the moving van arrives. Chris was a great sport. We sold his house and moved several times those first few years of sharing homes. One on the beach, one on the bay, and finally, we bought one on a golf course. The second year of my new sober life I discovered a new addiction, golf. A good friend, Joan, taught me everything she knew, and I progressed from wrapping a club around a tree to a decent game. I was surprisingly good at golf, and that probably had something to do with my genes and my marriage to the game. Chris did not play (his one and only match in Bermuda cinched that), and I continued to lower my handicap and excel. Life is good!

March 10, 1989
"My dear Janet.... I have sort of neglected you this last year, but then I didn't want to burden you with any of my problems for you have had enough for anyone.... I can't be at your ceremony as much as I would like to for it comes at a time that I can't get out of the clinic or leave my wife, who also is a patient with them. I wish you the best of all things in the years to come. You certainly deserve it for you have fought a very courageous battle, and from the invitation it appears that you have won it.... Chris is a lucky guy and I look forward to meeting him. You know my best wishes and prayers go with you in your new life. Love, Matt"

*　*　*

March 25, 1989, we married in a small ceremony in the same church where we met. All the children were in the wedding, and the reception was back at our new home overlooking the third fairway.

My baby sister, Lynn, was my maid of honor, and Chris's sponsor was his best man. No, my father did not give me away.

There was still a code of silence among his family members, and no one in the Admiral's family knew that I existed. Those were the conditions of our relationship. I was used to family secrets, which made this arrangement acceptable at the time.

We did meet in Florida with George, and I was so proud to introduce the Admiral to his grandson. Our correspondence during this time was all about new things, called feelings. Billy Joel wrote a song that year called "You're Only Human," and he told us that it is alright to make mistakes because we are only human. I wrote to the Admiral that even though I could not always identify which feelings I was having; it was great to have genuine emotion.

There were two more wonderful father and daughter meetings before the roof crashed down.

* * *

There is a saying in recovery circles that says something like this: "If things are going good, just wait, this too shall pass." Six months after we were married, I was taking courses at the local college to get my undergraduate degree, and I noticed that I was exhausted during the night classes. I also felt like I had the flu most of the time. With reluctance, I finally went to the family doctor. That would lead to a host of specialists with no answers and a steady decline in my health. Even my hair hurt, and it was difficult to get out of bed. Chris would try to touch me or kiss me, and it would be painful. I took a leave of absence from work, isolated from my sponsor and friends, experienced an overwhelming depression, and waited to die. I had one friend, our yellow Labrador, Alex. He stayed with me always, sat on the end of the bed, and did not like to leave my side. He had a way of curling up beside me and molding his warm furry body to mine without hurting me. It reminded me of my childhood fort in the dunes with Duke, my German Shepherd, protecting me and staying with me no matter what. Alex was our first Labrador Retriever of many to come.

Chris was beside himself and dragged me to one more medical specialist, a rheumatologist. The diagnosis was systemic lupus erythematosus. The prognosis was not very promising. I began a treatment of Prednisone, Plaquenil, and Prozac. The three Ps. Slowly, this new disease started to respond to the medications, and I made it down to the living room (where you are supposed to live). Unbeknownst to Chris, my first telephone call was to our minister, to tell him that I needed my marriage annulled because of this deadly disease, which would be too significant a burden on my husband. He listened, called Chris, and came to our house for a visit. We are still married.

There was a lot of fallout from lupus: I quit my job, I dropped out of school, I stopped playing golf, I let all the drama engulf me. When I did not bounce back as everyone had predicted, my mother ascended into town. She was living in California at the time and insisted that I get the best care possible. We flew to La Jolla, California, to the experts on lupus, Script's Institute. The trip was bizarre. I was dependent on my mother, which I had not been since I was five years of age, or ever. We had not spent more than five days together in twenty-five years. Finally, I had never forgiven her for the deception, the lies, and the life she had dished out for the past thirty years. Something big happened on this fortuitous journey.

Forgiveness does not always come in one fell swoop. My experience was just the opposite. It was gradual and reminded me of watching the tide go out at the beach. The water subsided oh so slowly, and if you stared at the tide line, it was hard to see the progression. However, over time, the waves were not coming in as far. The seaweed was further away from where I was sitting, and the sand fiddlers were sticking their heads out of holes that were once covered by water. Not drinking or drugging was giving me a fresh perspective on life, my friends, and my family.

*　*　*

Everyone blames their troubles, trials, and tribulations on their childhood, at least everyone born after Freud. I was no exception until I realized that I just did not have it that rough. At least I had a nest that I fell out of. I have met extraordinary people who had no parents, no home, and no love growing up. That was a bottom that I never hit. And yet, these courageous individuals survived, they prospered, and they loved themselves and others. These incredible triumphs of others caused me to look at my family and my mother differently.

My mother had a difficult childhood and wore the scars from her battles. She never had good mentors who taught her the values, ethics, and morals that are so important. She was a survivor and could only pass on to her kids what she was so freely given. It was time that I give my mother a break. I did not have to like her or who she wanted to be, but I could love her for who she was. This insight happened somewhere at 35,000 feet altitude above the Midwest plains. I am sure it was a long time formulating but there was that "aha" moment on that flight where I realized my mother was trying to save her daughter.

We landed in San Diego in late October. My mother had arranged to rent a car and to have a wheelchair meet our plane. We had a lot of time to kill before our appointment at Scripts so we decided to go to the San Diego Zoo. That seemed logical to both of us. However, my mother was exhausted, and pushing me in the wheelchair was taking its toll. No problem. We switched positions and rode the hills in the zoo with my mother in the seat and me standing on the back of our new chariot. Sometimes you just need to take risks, and we laughed until we cried. I never loved my mother more.

Three days at the hospital in California confirmed the lupus diagnosis, but their prognosis was much more optimistic, as it had not grossly affected my organs or my muscles. "Stay out of the sun and take your meds." That was the opposite of my psychiatrist's instructions. "Stay in the sun and take your meds." You just cannot win.

I visited my mother at her house in Santa Barbara for a week and returned home a new person with a new lease on life. My physical ailments were about the same, but I definitely felt like I had some kind of spiritual experience. I was not an orphan anymore. The tide was receding. The anger, the hate, and the burning resentments in my stomach were slowly subsiding. I told my sponsor and my husband that I was ready to start forgiving my mother and move on with my life. My sponsor responded with one sentence, "Why don't you forget the ready to start and just do it?"

* * *

One rare occasion, I called the Admiral. I told him about the lupus, my trip to the West Coast, and my visit with my mother. I think that I expected a congratulatory comment but I heard this: "Life is way too short to hold on to resentments. Tell your mother that you love her. Oh, please don't call me at this number."

August 6, 1991
"Dear Janet… I take it your mother now lives in California. You had a wonderful Christmas from what your letter says. I wonder if Alex

the dog is a Labrador for I have my 'girlfriend,' Virginia Belle, a nice yellow lab we got at the kennel in Middleburg, VA. I am the dog type not the cat kind! The Mayo clinic is only a short distance from where we live. Most people don't know they are located in Jacksonville as well as in Scottsdale and Rochester, Minnesota. They really have a plush set up and are real outstanding professionals in what they do. I guess I am a living testimony to that today. I will be eighty-three in November and have been operated on five times since 1986 when they first discovered my cancer. At the moment the cancer is in remission and I can even play golf if you call the 96 I shot golf. I swim and keep writing away on all the journals I kept during my life in the Navy and after. I couldn't do much for a while but am now up to where we go around the world in 1966, and I become President of a graduate school, Love, Matt"

September 7, 1991
"Dear Admiral... Yes, Alex is a yellow lab.... I knew you had to be the 'dog type'.... Is the cancer still in remission or what's the prognosis? My lupus has been in remission for about six months and it's wonderful not to be in pain all the time. You mentioned that you still play golf (me too) and that you shot a 96. Was that on the front nine or the back?
I am in a period of transition right now. Last Friday was my last day as a real estate broker and I ended a fifteen-year career in management. There was no challenge there anymore and I needed a change.... There is nothing holding us in Rehoboth and we want to make a move to the mountains next summer.... I would like to be near a university so I can go back and do some graduate studies.... The lupus is OK; I've been clean and sober for almost six years; my marriage is wonderful; and I really do not know what's next. One of the things that I want to

do is breed labs.... I am very serious about breeding labs and we need some land to do that. So, we are saving every penny that we can and will be selling our house here so we can buy up in the mountains.... I do want to see you and would like to know when and where is best for you. Chris and I will either fly or drive up north or to Florida whenever it is good for you and we can get away.

I did want to mention that my mother was just here for a visit and it was the nicest one ever.... Family is very important to me and I have never had one. Chris and I and our labs are probably as close as I will come. My children and I have a very good relationship, but it is distant, and their lives are totally separate from mine.

My oldest son, George, starts Colorado University at Boulder this year, and I am very proud of him. He is very intelligent, responsible, good-looking, and loves me very much. We talk once a week or so, and he is undecided as to what he wants to do with the rest of his life. George is very strong in the sciences (he gets that from his mom) and gets along extremely well with people. He has worked since he was fifteen and will blaze his own trail somewhere. George is just shy of six feet (unless you ask him his height), and has lost the sun-bleached blond hair that he had as a young tot. He has a beautiful smile that lights up my room. He is the serious one. I don't think his mind ever slows down and he challenges everyone on everything. 'Why would you do that, Mom? How does that really work? Why do you say that?' It is scary how smart he really is. George really does not like to hug and when I embrace him he is very stiff. I do not know when that started, but I do hope that changes and he will be soft and cuddly again.

My middle son, David, is sixteen and a straight 'A' student in high school in Colorado. He is my sensitive one and we are very close. His bright-red, orangey hair sets him apart in the family, in the world. His hair is usually unkempt and going twenty different directions at any given time. There are lots of freckles and I love every one of them. David was born with a special gift. Since second grade he has been sketching very detailed drawings on a scratch pad. In third grade he was selected to attend a special school for the artistically gifted and talented. Going to those classes sparked David's creativity and he began drawing comic characters, which he invented, and people that he saw in his life travels. Much to the chagrin of his older brother, my red-headed son towers over six feet tall. He lost all his baby fat in his teens and is very thin. David has very few close friends but has a reputation for being a really nice guy. He is attracted to quiet kids like himself and hangs around the nerds and the geeks most of the time. His arms are very long, and when he puts them around me, I feel very safe. David plays soccer like his brother but never takes it too seriously and probably plays so he could be more like George. He worships his older brother and tries to do everything that he does, but better. That is a hard act to follow. I remember when he was six, he tried to ride his two-wheeler (no training wheels) down the driveway to catch up with his brother. There was a crash into the mailbox and David ended up with a cracked jaw. Fortunately, it was not too serious and healed on its own. As a youngster, David cried easily and bounced back way too fast. Maybe he does wear his emotions on his sleeve.

Then, there is Kate, my fourteen-year-old daughter. There is something special between mothers and daughters and it is not always smooth sailing. Kate came to visit for five weeks this summer and we got along extremely well, but she is having all kinds of problems with her father, Wes, in Colorado. I don't know what the future holds for Kate. Following her older brother, Kate also has beautiful red hair. Hers is softer and has some blond overtones. Her hair is gorgeous and full of natural curls. There are fewer freckles and she never has had the acne problems which plagued her brothers. Kate also played soccer and her first game set the stage for her future role in sports. The referee blew the whistle for Kate's first game to begin. Since she was on the front line, she was face to face with the opposing team. Recognizing one of her playmates from school, she and this little boy on the other team walked over to each other, held hands, and together sauntered over the sideline into a field of daisies. Her personality was alive and well at age five. Kate also does well in school, but she has to work for it. She is every bit as smart as her older brothers, but she is easily distracted. With lots of friends and more important things to do except study, Kate does have constant altercations with her father over grades. Adolescence is tough and is becoming more difficult for Kate as her self-esteem decreases and her weight increases. She is overweight and uses food like any addictive drug. I love her dearly and don't know what more I can do for her other than continuously pray for her, which I do…. I feel safe telling you these things and hope you will write back soon. Love, Janet"

*　*　*

The following summer, Chris retired from the Coast Guard. Since I had already left the real estate field, we decided to make the major move and trade the ocean for the mountains. Moving away from the beach was a big decision, but it was calculated and seemed to satisfy all the immediate goals that we had for our life together. I wanted to go to graduate school, and Chris wanted to launch a new career teaching in a middle school. That is how we ended up in our new home in the Appalachians.

Before our moving, Kate made a special request. She wanted to leave her father's house and live with us. Everyone agreed, and I was ecstatic. Being separated from my children was a loss that had been unbearable at times. I would fly out to Colorado, book a hotel room with an indoor pool, and we would spend time together having fun. In good weather we would hike the trails, and on a couple of occasions, we rode horses in state parks that were close to their father's home. I made multiple visits each year to see them, and each trip tore me up when I had to end our time together. Chris helped through the years with the emotional turmoil, and his acceptance of Kate was a gift.

* * *

The *Big Move!* After making a couple of trips to visit southwest Virginia, we ended our area search and settled for a location around Blacksburg and the Virginia Tech University. Chris attended several teaching interviews and was hired as a fourth grade elementary school teacher. He would be the only male teacher in his new school and one of the few in the county.

Having a real estate background, I was specific with the real estate agent as to what kind of home we were seeking. It had to have two stories, four bedrooms, a fireplace, maybe a hot tub, and a fenced yard of at least one-quarter acre. After an exhaustive search with no success, the agent announced that there was a new home on the market in the country and that we might want to see. There was a long gravel driveway, and you could not see the house from the road. We passed a small barn and continued down the drive to the most spectacular view we had ever seen. It was a 360-degree view of mountains with no neighbors and lots of pasture and trees. We fell in love instantly and broke all the rules by showing our agent how motivated we were to buy. Did I mention that it was a two-year-old ranch home with three bedrooms, no fireplace, no hot tub and included twenty-eight acres of gorgeous land? We drove around the back of the property and someone somewhere said, "Cue the deer." A family of four, including two fawns, was standing on a back road to the farm. That did it! We did look at the house but really did not care about the details, since we would have been willing to pitch a tent to own this property. Two days later it was ours. It would be almost two months to the day, after our family vacation, that we would move in. Chris and I are still here twenty-eight years later.

Before settling into our new location, Chris, Kate, and I decided to tour the United States. Packing a Ford Explorer and a pop-up camper with our daughter, three Labradors, and all our gear was a challenge, but we did it. We were towing the camper that we had rented in Rehoboth Beach. I had lots of experience towing boats and could even master backing up. You just do the opposite of what you think you should do and that camper whips around where it wants to go. Piece of cake! It took quite a number of practice runs, but we did master camper 101.

We had two months to spend on the road in awfully close quarters. This trip would make us or break us. Traveling is always an adventure, and who would have guessed what awaited us around the next bend?

One of the highlights of our trip was visiting our boys in Las Cruces, New Mexico. Our oldest son had moved there with his finance to finish his undergraduate program, and our youngest son enrolled part-time to begin his studies. It was the middle of July, and we were all ready to take a break from camping, check into an air-conditioned hotel, and have a few days off the highway. This family reunion was going to be unique with all the kids and three dogs in one place. We met the boys early in the morning at our hotel so we could all go out to breakfast and catch up on everyone's life. Simple plan, right? We were sitting in the room visiting with Alex, Briana, and Calli, our canine kids, and I asked George to please go start our car to cool it down. Then we could move the dogs to their nesting spot in the back of the Ford. George came back to the room with the car keys and asked where it was parked. I gave him my "you are not that stupid" look and told him that it was right at the end of the short walkway immediately in front of our hotel room. "Mom, it is not there." Finally, we confirmed that it had vanished from the parking lot.

Chris asked the policeman when he thought they could recover our stolen car. I will never forget that laugh. He was very polite and informed us, "Your Ford Explorer is already in 10,000 pieces across the Mexican border and you will never see it again." Yes, we were grateful that the dogs were not in it and we had unhooked the pop-up camper, but what were we going to do? The insurance money would not kick in for thirty days, and no one would rent us a car or truck when we disclosed that we were pulling a camper. Our summer trip had undoubtedly hit a snag. Thank God that I was sober and was flying straight so this event did not become another crisis.

It really does help to have an eccentric mother that can be heroic and thinks outside of the box. When my mother heard our dilemma, she offered to drive her pickup truck from California to Las Cruces and lend it to us until we were able to buy a new car. She flew back to her home in Santa Barbara, and we were once more on our way. The entire episode made for a great family saga, and you can still hear the embellished version from time to time.

There were other highlights of that summer vacation that are worth mentioning. I did most of the driving across the country, and Chris was the navigator. Kate kept an eye on the dogs and provided a great sense of humor. The seating arrangement was entirely different from the Ford to the Chevy pickup. We had a cap over the back end of the truck, but there was still six inches between the truck cab and the rear end. It made it very noisy in the back, not as cool as the front. It was hot! There were three of us and only a bench seat up front for the driver and one passenger. That was a challenge. Ingenuity does run in my family. Since one of us was going to be riding in the back with the dogs, we purchased a comfortable lawn chair, cut off the chair legs to create enough headroom, and bought a thick pad for nap times. There was still one big problem. You could not hear the people in the front if you were in the back, and the dogs were still not talking. It got kind of lonely back there. Surely you have heard of putting a string between two cans and talking to each other by holding the can up to your ear. We did not do that. I still am not sure who had that brilliant idea. We took a ten-foot piece of plastic dryer venting hose and ran it between the front seat and the person sitting in the rear. Not only could we talk to each other, but we could hear the radio and get a little air from the front to the back. It was creative and did the trick.

Enough about transportation. During our summer vacation, the Labradors learned many new tricks. They stood in line with all the other children to get their picture taken in front of the Yosemite State Park sign. We took long hikes and only got lost on one trail one time. Dogs like to swim, and our all our dog's web feet were there for a reason. The two yellow labs with their one black sister visited lakes, streams, and even the Pacific Ocean that summer. There was one incident worth reporting. We had stopped for a lunch break along the side of the road and realized that there was a beautiful stream running behind the rest area. Chris picked up a stick and gave it a toss. After all, our dogs were retrievers. Unfortunately, that was not a little stream, but a very fast-moving rapid, and all three dogs were in the water before we realized the danger. None of our dogs could swim against the current, and they were being dragged downstream quickly. I could see some class 2 rapids in their path and immediately began to wade to intersect their drift. Kate ran downstream with a rope, in case Chris and I could not catch the dogs. We were in the middle of a crisis and did not consider our own safety first. This does have a happy ending. I believe that my "higher power" loved dogs and worked anonymously that day to save them and us. There was a slight bend in the river before the faster moving water, and all three dogs were able to swim to this little eddy where we could reach them. We kept all retrieving sticks on land from that day forward.

Somewhere in Montana, Chris began complaining about the stomach flu and just feeling crummy. We put him in the back with the dogs and started covering a lot of miles in one day. In fact, the whole trip from Montana to Virginia was a blur, and our Chevy truck crossed state lines in record time. We really thought Chris would improve and reaching our destination would be much better for him. But that was not the case.

It was too early to take possession of our new home, so we holed up in a hotel. Finding a doctor was not difficult, and the diagnosis for Chris was a kidney infection. The prognosis was excellent, and the antibiotics put him back on his feet in three days. It was time to move into our new house.

Chris had recuperated, and the moving van was arriving the next day. We decided to take possession of our new home and camp out with no electricity, but the water had been turned on. The three Labradors checked out every vacant room and ran out the back door the first opportunity that they had. Everything inside had been freshly painted, the floors sparkled, and the garage was huge. We were all overly excited and could not believe that we had this beautiful home, our farm, and the breathtaking views. It was starting to get dark when we realized that the dogs were still outside. Our kitchen was about to be christened.

Shouts and whistles did not bring the dogs home. We decided to split up and start the search. Alex and Briana were in the pasture that belonged to our closest neighbor, but there was no sign of Callie. It was time to drag out the flashlights, split up, and find the youngest canine. I have two reactions when one of the dogs wanders off. When we do reunite, I am so happy, and I want to kill 'em. Well, Callie could not be found, and we were getting apprehensive. I heard Kate yell, "I found her!" Chris and I were in the kitchen, and Callie came running in and shaking her coat vigorously. That was a mystery, since it wasn't raining. Why was she jumping around and throwing her tail back and forth? The white walls were splattered with red, and we realized that Callie had been shot. We still do not know who the perpetrator was but had a few ideas. She did look like a coyote with her long red-yellow coat, and most of the farms around us have young calves that needed to be protected. The good news is that it was birdshot. We threw her in the bathtub and picked out as many metal pellets as possible. We spent a couple hours at the veterinarian hospital and were told that Callie was lucky, since her face was not shot and most of her wounds were superficial. That is how we spent our first night in our new home.

* * *

I do not know when I started counting, but until we settled in our mountain retreat, I had lived in over twenty different houses. None of them were home. It did not have anything to do with a two-story, being a ranch, having a pool, not having a fireplace, being in the woods, or on the waterfront. Home really is where the heart is. Now, granted, that first night and that first year on the farm had its challenges. Our daughter decided she did not want to go to a high school next to a cow pasture. Chris's teaching job was a forty-five-minute commute instead of the twenty minutes he thought. I had decided to pursue an education in the counseling field and was enrolled at Virginia Tech. Going to graduate school required twice as much time and effort than I had expected. Finally, we all realized that running a small farm would have to be a joint effort. There were some compromises, and everyone began to settle down. We were on a new journey, and no one was exactly sure of the destination.

* * *

Letters from the Admiral were unquestionably different. He began to report on his children and his nine grandchildren. The paragraphs were in-depth descriptions of his relationship with his wife and all the accomplishments that his five (does not include me) children were making. It sounded like everyone in his family were super-achievers and hugely successful. What was interesting is that I was jealous. That ugly emotion had reared its head before, and I did not like it. It felt like being mired in quicksand and not being able to do anything. I kept sinking, and the more that I wallowed in the envy, the more helpless and hopeless I felt. *What about me? I am a super-achiever. Are you proud of me?* I decided to call him and ignore one of his rules, "Never call."

January 1, 1992
"My dear Janet… The phone call was at a time when we were involved in some serious problem discussion with one of the grandchildren. I would prefer you didn't call. I believe I understand how you feel about the situation, but you must look at the problem from all angles. There is a lapse of over thirty years in any of our contacts prior to our first meeting. I have been married for sixty years this year. It hasn't been

all moonlight and roses, but I love her and have loved her over the years. I am not proud of my actions but then I guess that is life.... She is eighty-one years old and it has not been an easy life being married to me, I am sure. However, I am not giving up as yet and don't bury me yet.

Contrary to your belief, I feel I understand your feeling and will do my best to help. I will certainly arrange to see you and your husband and talk with you, and it will probably help both of us.... I would love to meet you in Washington again. I could spend the good part of the day with you and would suggest we meet at the Army Navy Club on Farragut Square about ten o'clock that morning, 14th February, Friday. I will be waiting there, and if for any reason you can't make it, you could call the desk and leave a message for me. I will keep the whole day free and we can talk and do a little bit of sightseeing or whatever you desire.... It is not an easy situation for either one of us, and I am very sorry that years ago that there was no communication or solutions—it sure would have simplified problems then from what they are now. Anyway that has been overtaken by events and there is little good in going into all the problems and background.... Unless I hear otherwise, I will see you in Washington on the 14th of February. See you Valentine's Day. Love, Matt"

    The visit was short, but I was so proud to introduce Chris to the Admiral. Watching them discuss military stuff was a dream come true. Two of my most favorite men (my two sons being the others) were in front of me, trying to get to know each other. It was a rare audience and both men kept me involved with the conversation. We talked about breeding Labradors, teachers of all kinds, the counseling field, staying educated, and end-of-life realities. The Admiral looked worn out, wrinkled and yet he shared the best part of him, his love for his family and his rare trait of remaining teachable, wanting to learn more. After lunch, Chris and I went back to the hotel quietly. I needed to decompress, to take in the whole experience, and to revel in all that had taken place. I did not know if I would ever see my father again, but I did get some closure during this visit. Having Chris present was so special. Now, the gates had been opened, and I could share all my feelings with my best friend. We headed home the next morning, and even though there was a sense of loss, I was grateful. I still had a lot to learn and even more to process, but my father–daughter time was worth every minute. We drove home without the radio blaring and talked about missing our dogs.

* * *

Like some of you, I grew up watching *The Waltons* on television and was thoroughly convinced that saying goodnight to John Boy was how a family lived happily and created a home. I maintained this idea of everyone being under one roof as the prerequisite to happy, especially during the holidays. That first Christmas in our new home was a huge disappointment. George did not come to our house for the holidays. He had his own family and spent time with his in-laws. David had other plans and promised to come for a visit during spring break. My father did not have time for a visit, and my mother was still living on the West Coast. Chris's family was always very aloof, and no one met my expectations. That is when I discovered that it really was best to make plans but not to plan the outcome. My expectations were totally unrealistic, but there was some magic in the air.

Slowly, I realized that I needed to relax and enjoy what I had. *What happened to live in the moment?* Spirituality is not an event but a process, and it can be magical. Once I straightened out my priorities, I became much more accepting and finally, loving. After all, I now had my daughter living with us, a husband who adored me, and three crazy Labradors that were about to become parents. Our house was beginning to feel like "home."

* * *

Kate joined her high school tennis team, got her driver's license, and started making friends. Chris settled into teaching fourth grade and became an instant success. Not only was he one of the few male teachers, but he was special and took the kids out of the books and into the real world, teaching them how to think. There were family histories, building a dog sled for the Iditarod (using our Labradors as Huskies), and other projects which made learning fun and creative.

I mentioned that graduate school was time-consuming, and it was also a major challenge. I took courses like statistics that almost did me in. Fortunately, I found a tutor who was a math genius and he walked me through the class and together, we passed the final exam. Most of the courses were extremely interesting and I was like a sponge soaking up new knowledge. I not only devoured the recommended reading list but asked for more information from my instructors. The faculty were top-notch and were interested in giving me the best training possible. It was an exciting time to be in graduate school at the local university and launch my new counseling career. My whole family was so proud of me, and David traveled from New Mexico to attend my graduation. That was an extraordinary day, and I was beginning to believe in miracles. During those first few years at my new home and after our last visit to Washington, D.C., there was little contact with my father.

December 6, 1993

"Dear Janet... Congratulations! I know you must have worked hard to get it for VPI is not an easy school.... I know how difficult it is to go back to school after one has been out a while. It took me about twelve years of being a tramp scholar at many a university to finally get what I wanted.

Can't say that I approve very much of the present administration's approach to the foreign policy business. I believe Clinton is a loser and wouldn't turn litmus paper. The world is a dangerous place and we better keep our powder dry and make up our mind what our objectives are before charging off in all directions.

This is just a quick note to tell you how glad I am for you to have gotten your master's. I will write more later. Love, Matt"

* * *

The following summer I took a trip to visit my boys in Las Cruces. George and his wife were still in school. As I mentioned earlier, David had moved to New Mexico and was supposedly taking classes. It did not take long to figure out that David was majoring in golf discus and had dropped out of college. He seemed lost, and I do not know what was really going on in his life. I never met any of his friends and had no idea where he was living when he was not with his older brother. There were so many questions and very few answers. I just wanted to spend time with him.

My red-headed son was so tall. *When did he grow taller than his brother?* David was so skinny, and his legs were covered with red hair. His arms were so long. *Where did he get those muscles in those biceps?* I wanted to bring him home with me. I felt like we had lost that close mother–son bond, or did we ever have that? On the inside I was crying that we were not in tune with each other's feelings or thoughts. *Does this happen to sons and not daughters? Is it my fault, and will I ever get rid of the guilt that this is permanent and cannot be reversed?*

Wanting to extend my visit, I devised a plan which would hopefully intensify our relationship and pull us closer together. David and I took a spur-of-the-moment bus ride to Juarez, Mexico. It was a lunch tour of the city. We laughed on the ride down, and I could hear his heart singing when he talked about past vacations we had taken when he was a child.

Oh, I relished those moments and was trying to figure out how to extend that trip indefinitely. It was only a two-hour trip across the border, and I saw all the poverty in Mexico from the bus. We arrived mid-morning and signed up for the walking tour of Juarez, which culminated at an incredible touristy restaurant with pinatas hanging everywhere and waiters speaking perfect English. David and I shared a look of disbelief that we were not in Mexico but had been transported to a very gaudy Mexican restaurant in the old U.S. It did not matter, as I was with my son and I wanted that moment to last forever.

I bought a souvenir sweatshirt with the name of the restaurant, Chihuahua Charlie's, on the front so I could remember that incredible day together. I had never been to Mexico and would never return. Little did I know that that would be the last time I would see my son. Our world was about to come crashing down.

* * *

Late in October, I got the phone call that no parent ever wants to receive. My son David had been arrested in Mexico for using peyote and being drunk in public. No damage had been done so he was transferred to an American sheriff at the Texas border. The call was from a detective who told us that David was being taken to a shelter for the night and we could talk to him the next morning. I made plans to fly to Texas and bring him home to sort out the mess. I telephoned his father and suggested he help in some way. Being an attorney, certainly he could get David out of this predicament. His response was: "He is not welcome here. When he turned eighteen, he knew that he was on his own." Early the next morning, the puzzle unraveled, and we will never know what really happened. David left the shelter in the middle of the night, and his location was unknown. It was all beginning to sound like an evil Law and Order.

October 23, 1995, we got the most devastating call ever. They had found a body by the railroad tracks, and the identification would have to be verified using dental records. The detective was 90 percent sure that it was our David. I collapsed in the bedroom and the next four days were a total blur. Everything from that telephone call forward became a living nightmare.

I do not remember the sequence of events, but I was sitting on my bed in some kind of unbelievable trance. Time seemed to stand still. My daughter was sitting next to me and my husband was talking. "What is he saying? Why is everyone crying?" I did not want to move, as just standing might have made that unbelievably bad nightmare real. I saw several of our Labradors on the carpet and suggested to Chris that he needed to feed the dogs. That was just like the *Twilight Zone*, where after the commercial, things surely return to normal. *What is normal? Why is everyone talking in platitudes?*

The local Methodist minister came to the house, and I do remember sitting in my bedroom staring at her as she prayed and began to take over the situation. Chris, Kate, and I were so lost and did not know what to do.

Looking back, our reactions and what followed in the next few days were all devoid of emotion, and everyone looked and acted like the walking dead, zombies. There was a funeral, but there was no body. David had been cremated because of the horrific condition of the accident. He had been run over by a train. *Suicide or murder?* was the question, and everyone but me seemed to have an answer. *Was he depressed? Was the peyote responsible for the outcome? Was he murdered by a known drug cartel that had killed in that area before?* There was no one to blame, no one to yell at, and no one who had any conclusive answers. It would take a decade to stop asking those questions and just accept that David was gone. But the hole in my heart would never go away.

Kate, Lynn, and I were sitting on a double bed in a motel room. There was a man taking notes, and I found out later that he was the minister who would do the funeral service. He had a memo pad and was writing down information that Lynn and Kate were sharing with him. *Who is he? Who are they talking about?* I do remember thinking that they were all wrong but I have no idea about the answers they were giving the man. They were telling the strange man what David liked to do, what his hobbies were, and were describing David's physical characteristics. *Why is this man not asking me about my own son? Why are they talking about my son in the past tense?*

The only other memory is one incident from the memorial service. Chris was embracing Wes, my first husband, and they were both sobbing. I wondered why they were so upset and how strange it was that they were trying to comfort each other. I still have that picture etched in my mind. I guess a mother can only handle so much.

We flew back home and tried to pretend that life would go on as always. Not for me. My life stopped, and there were no words, no hugs, and no medications that would repair the colossal defect in my heart. I could not talk about it and was not ready to accept the loss. I stopped all contact with my AA group, did not go to recovery meetings, did not call my AA sponsor, and made excuses not to see friends or anyone. I stopped writing to my father and refused to talk to my mother. My mother was not doing anything to make the situation bearable and I was not going to give her the chance to make me feel worse. If someone asked how I was doing, my standard answer was "Fine." It would be years before the emotional pain escaped. I felt just like I did when I was nineteen, hopeless, very depressed, numb, and all alone. Not even a father could fix this traumatic time in my life.

January 29, 1997
"Dear Janet… I guess the road to hell is paved with good intentions for I have intended to write long before this. I know just how David's death must have crushed you. There is little to say to anyone that has had such a tragic blow. I am so old I just do not understand the youth of today. The sad part is to realize how discouraged and hurt he was to take his own life. I guess no one could have helped him. All we can do is pray for him.
My life has been full of tragedies these last years but I am not one to tell all my troubles to the world, but times are hard…. We are here in our little house by the sea and probably will never go back north. We both need twenty-four hours around-the-clock care, and my wife is bedridden most of the time. I can drive in the day only. My cancer treatment is still on going and we both go to the Mayo Clinic here in Florida. I get a bone scan every sixty days. I turned up with a broken neck from an early accident and have lost most of the use of my left arm. My titanium leg is still doing ok, but I stagger around a bit when I walk. Any way you look at it, old age is the pits.

I wish this could be a more pleasant letter but then I knew I should write and tell you all that has happened but always put it off. You had your own problems, and there was little use in telling mine. This is no excuse for not writing but maybe I did give up.

I pray all the time that I can do what has to be done. I just hope the good I have done in my life will outweigh the bad but really do not know if that will happen.

I look at some of the things I wrote over the years and wonder how it all came about. In my diary in 1930, I wrote on the first page: ""There is room in the halls of pleasure / For a long Lordly train / But one by one we must all file on / Through the narrow Aisles of pain." Another entry was: "We hope, we resolve, we aspire, we pray / And we think that we mount the air on wings / Beyond the call of sensual things / While our feet still cling to the heavy clay." I guess I was a very serious young man in those days but am so glad I kept a journal over all those years in the Navy.

Anyway, I will do better on writing and letting you know how things are going with us. Please give Chris my regards. I know you know how hard it was for me to write this letter, but now I am glad I finally came around to do it. Love, Matt"

It took fifteen months after my son's death for the Admiral to write to me. Procrastination, denial, fear—they are indeed the opposite of persistence. In the last letter, my father had decided my son's death was a suicide, his current life was a tragedy, and there was nothing he could do to make me feel better. He was right about the last conclusion!

Chapter 6: Surviving

Life did resume after David's death, and we all took up from where we had left off. Chris went back to teaching, Kate went back to high school, and I just went to our house. Sadly, it no longer felt like home. I could not look at family photos, and I kept my souvenir sweatshirt from Mexico hanging in my closet. It would hold its place of honor at the end of the sweater section for the next twenty-plus years. I never could bring myself to wear it and often feared that the white would turn yellow or that the lettering would deteriorate as time went on. The only personal item that the police saved for us when they found David was a sketch pad. What a gift and a curse! I wanted to hold it, to look at all his drawings and I never wanted to see it again. I was so confused and just wanted my son back.

It was about this time that I began having severe physical problems. An old back injury from my thirties, from waterskiing "high" and hitting a beach, showed its ugly head. I had to go to the University of Virginia and have the chief of neurosurgery perform my second back surgery. All went well, but physical recovery was prolonged.

Any time that I am restricted physically, the results are complicated by my mental illness. My bipolar disorder rears its ugly head and the added stress sends me into a tailspin of suicidal depression or a mixed state where the mood swings skyrocket out of control. It is challenging to be manic or hypomanic and not be able to move around. It's like trying to throw a stick for one of our Labradors and holding him back so he cannot do the retrieving that he is bred to do. Unfortunately, during those manic times, I would often go beyond the limits of my body and do harm to my joints, muscles, or bones. Mania is not my friend. Family and friends would often remark how lucky I was to have the energy to clean my whole house in two hours or cut four acres of grass in less than three. True. I did like those moods and bursts of energy, as I could get so much done. The price I paid was debilitating. During those high mood swings, I also hiked too far, skied on too tricky slopes, played twenty-four holes of golf, and risked too much. During the next two decades, I would have another back surgery, a right knee arthroscopic surgery, operations on both shoulders, and a serious neck surgery. Fortunately, my systemic lupus diagnosed nine years earlier was in remission. Due to my drinking and drugging in my twenties and thirties, I had destroyed my digestive system. Over time, I would have to have a colon resection, an esophagus relining, a gallbladder removed, and a special diet to accommodate diverticulitis and acid reflux. It is utterly amazing how resilient our body is, and I really do try today not to abuse it. I had to learn my limits if I was going to accomplish any of my goals.

* * *

Having completed my graduate studies, it was time to look for a job. I was hired to be a school counselor in an elementary school. Life was a play, and I began acting the parts that were expected. My role as mother, wife, and employee started again. I had a few new friends, and they were trying to give me emotional support. I remained sober, if that describes an empty life void of being happy, joyous, or free. David's death hung over me like a black cloak. I did not drink or return to my drug addiction, but I could best be described as being on a "dry drunk." I am not proud of that time in my life because I was totally self-absorbed and was not there for anyone else, even my family. God knows that they tried to reach me, to help, but the pain was too big for any of us. Chris and I attended a support group called Compassionate Friends that was meeting once a month to help parents who had lost a child. I wanted to cry in those meetings, but the tears that I felt burning my eyes would not come out. My David was not lost. He was dead. The euphemisms I heard made me angry. Almost everything made me angry. It was the only emotion that made sense, and I stayed stuck in that stage of grief. Occasionally, I would move into a deep depression and then back to my comfortable feeling of self-righteous anger. One of my friends said to me, "At least you have two other children." I did not talk to her for an exceedingly long period.

* * *

The following fall we decided to breed the Labradors that we owned and sell the puppies. We had plenty of acreage, a large room in the back of the garage to house all those dogs, and a library that would serve as the whelping room. It was too bad that all the excitement and joy looked incredible on the outside. However, my outsides did not match my insides. The bipolar disease was running rampant.

Living with mental illness affects not only me but my entire family. The psychiatrist could not find the medication that would control my rapid mood cycling. I never knew who I was going to be when I awakened in the morning. I would look at Chris lying beside me and wondered when he was going to take off and put my family and me behind him. The issue of abandonment surfaced big time, and I just expected him to leave me. The only question was when? There were only the extremes, very manic or very depressed. I was continually performing by trying to be someone stable that had a full-time school counselling job, a functional family, and a side job of breeding puppies. Something had to break.

*　*　*

During lunch or after school I would drive down to park by the lake and stop to smoke a cigarette or burn the butt into my arm. Other coworkers would decide where to go have lunch, and I would decide on the self-mutilation for the day. I would contemplate the most accessible form of suicide and watch the clock, so I would get back to work on time. I saw a counselor, visited with the psychiatrist, and told everyone that everything was "fine."

Denial is a compelling state of mind, and I had no idea just how powerful the act of minimizing or ignoring the symptoms could be. It did not help that I was lying by omission to everyone. Finally, the counselor got to the truth and demanded that I go to the local psychiatric hospital immediately. By local, I mean one hour from our house, as I certainly did not want anyone to know that I was crazy.

Psychiatric hospitals are unique in that almost no one wants to be there. Everyone lies about why they are there, and there is a dark cloud that convinces most residents that they are there by mistake. I was no exception and was not compliant with the routine. The staff kept telling me to get with the program. What program? Speaking up in group sessions, not isolating in your room, and taking your medicine as prescribed are prerequisites for getting out. In my case, the program was not working. It was time for drastic measures. I gave up.

*　*　*

One out of five persons experiences depression in their lifetime. Normally (that is an ambiguous word), this brain disorder can be treated with anti-depressants. However, I was "unaverage" and one of the exceptions. Different medications still had little or no effect on my depression. It was time for electroconvulsive shock therapy, or ECT for short. After a series of eight ECT treatments, I was released from the hospital and scheduled to return for four more ECT sessions. Yes, this treatment is still very controversial, but it saved my life. The details are just not important. My family got Janet back. I was able to return to work. The miracle is that I still stayed sober through that experience and was able to get back into a program of recovery. My lupus remained in remission. It would not be my last hospitalization or my last ECT treatment.

Mania is a two-headed dragon. Let us just say that I got a lot done in a short period of time. I became the superwoman, needed little sleep, and accomplished what most people only dreamed of achieving. Unfortunately, at the same time, I was continuing to wear out my body physically and would end up collapsing from fatigue at some point, usually four to six weeks in the manic cycle. Depression always followed, and ECT would come shortly after that. Often, I would lose one or two days after the shock therapy. It does require general anesthesia, makes you very lethargic, takes your short- and long-term memory away, and would give me a crushing headache. Thank God for Dilaudid! It would help with the post-trauma of ECT and be given to me in the hospital so as not to interfere with my drug addiction issues. I did not ever discuss the pain of losing my son, but I survived.

***

My experience in the parking lot at our local grocery store did help. I was putting plastic bags in the trunk and heard David say, "Mom." I whipped around to find him, and he was not there. I know it was David and he spoke to me. I did not tell anyone about the experience, as I knew everyone would write it off as being "crazy." It was David.

I believe that to this day. There is an afterlife, and my son is part of it. He is somewhere, and I just want to be there.

*　*　*

By this time, I was overcome with self-pity and self-loathing. I was still practicing self-injurious behavior and pretending that everything was alright. I wore a thick mask and would not let anyone into my world. However, my father's correspondence helped more than he would ever know.

March 3, 1997
"Dear Janet… Distressed to hear of your illness. I hope this finds you back on an even keel. George seems to be doing real well and I know he must be enjoying what he is involved in at the university. I have no real knowledge of how they treat you but have read considerably on the subject of manic depression. I feel very depressed at times myself but have never taken anything for it…. I try to grow old gracefully not telling anyone of my aches and pains and going about my business. I do enjoy my charity work at the children's hospital. I feel so sorry for some of those children who are retarded, but we do get excellent results in our work with them. It's the single-parent families that are in the worst condition. Anyway, I spend a day down there every time I can, which is about once a week….Get well in a hurry. Love, Matt"

January 28, 1998

"Dear Janet… I do have a must engagement in Washington on the 3rd and 4th of March. I am pretty crippled but will be there, as I have to make a meeting where I am a trustee and must settle some affairs by the board of one of the people involved who died recently. The doctors say I will be able to make it. I will be staying at the Army Navy Club on Farragut Square. I would love to have lunch with you on the 4th at 12.30 if you can meet me there. I will let you know if anything should change but at this time do not think anything will happen to change it.

I can tell you I am persisting and am sure you know just how depressed I am with my wife's condition. There is little hope for her I realize but then we have been married sixty-five years and I will embrace the challenge…. Hope you can make it. As ever, Matt"

February 8, 1998

"Dear Admiral… I am anxious to see you in Washington on March 4th and will meet you at the Army/Navy Club at 12:30 pm. I am surprised that you can make the trip and hope that is a good decision on your part…. I just surprised Chris with a big birthday party on his fiftieth and he says that he had no idea. I guess that I am still a good liar. Work is going pretty well but I am extremely busy and having some difficulty balancing work with other commitments. I know that is a lifelong process. I think that it is really neat that you stay so active at your age and still can take care of your wife and yourself. That is inspiration for me. Love, Janet"

* * *

I forgot to mention that I was using the revolving door at the psychiatric hospital. I was receiving ECT treatments every month, called maintenance ECT, and every few months was involuntarily checked into the hospital for erratic, manic, or depressive behavior. Not only was I working on balance in my life, but I was still struggling with survival. I was extremely suicidal during this period and spent a great deal of time hiding that from my spouse, my supervisor, my children, and my therapist. Thank God, I was a mediocre actor and action was taken to keep me safe.

* * *

Cognition is a tricky thing. With all the ECT treatments, not only was my memory affected, but I was having difficulty reading. I would read a paragraph and have no idea what I read and would have to reread several times to just grasp the message. My psychiatrist referred me to Johns Hopkins Hospital in Maryland to get a full work-up. The diagnosis: "You have a bipolar disorder and should continue the ECT on a monthly maintenance schedule, continue with the prescribed medications, and try to have less stress in your life." A very tall order with no surprises. The day that I was discharged, we heard good news that my brain had not been fried. That was the conclusion of the visit. I went home depressed and seriously questioned my future. It was too bad that I was still not talking the truth to anyone and worked so hard to hide my numbness and my lack of motivation to go forward.

* * *

February 17, 1998

"Dear Janet.... My wife died on Saturday morning and I am pretty devastated and will have a lot to do, so if you do not, repeat not, hear from me, do not be in Washington on the 4th, as my schedule is really upset at the moment. Regards, Matt"

Now he was signing his letter with "Regards." It was clear that my father was not going to be any support or help for me. There I go again, thinking the whole world revolved around me. Self-pity is really overrated. It is like a tick embedded in your skin. It can go unnoticed, but it eats at you and causes constant irritation. Despite self-absorption, I did plan a trip to visit my eldest son in Florida and did arrange a lunch with the Admiral to meet George.

April 19, 1998

"Dear Admiral... I hope your treatments are going OK. George and I had a wonderful lunch with you. Thank you for showing us Ponte Verde and the good company that we enjoyed. George was quite impressed with you. Not only in who you are and what you have done, but he told me on the drive back that you were the oldest person that he had ever talked to. I laughed and smiled on the inside. You are just so interesting and sharp for your age—it is refreshing. I hope I stay that way as I get older.

Please write and let me know how you are doing. We are all thinking about you up here. Love, Janet"

April 28, 1998

"Dear Janet... I am gld (sic) to have seen George and listen to his ideas he is an impressive young manand (sic) I am sure he will enjoy Gainesville. It is quite an impressive place. I did a lot of engineering business in the nuclear area with them years ago. I amon (sic) chemotherapy now and it is not pleasant, have some critical dates ahead, the 24th and 27th of this month. I go to Pensacola to be inducted into an honorable position by the Navy. I will be flown over and then return here eearly (sic) the next day. The Doctor said I could go. You really looked fine and in ggood (sic) health and I hope the lupus has fled. I hope you will let me know when you do come down again to Florida. Best to George and Chris and yourself Love"

The visit with the Admiral and my son was definitely a shot in the arm for me. It brought me back to recovery. Through all the turmoil I had stayed sober with no alcohol or unprescribed drugs for twelve years. It was time to go back to meetings, get a sponsor, and practice honesty with my therapist. My son was expecting his first child in October (my first grandchild) and I wanted to be there for him. I had a job that was both challenging and rewarding. It was time to get my act together.

May 31, 1998
"Dear Matt… I thought that I would drop you a line and catch you up on the Virginia news. We only have eight more days of school, and I cannot wait for the break. I worked in the yard and garden all weekend and really am looking forward to more time outside. We now have four cows (two moms and two calves) in our front pasture. A farmer lends us the cows every summer, so they have a place to graze and we keep down the hay.
I have decided to work this summer in a reading and math camp our school has here for the neediest kids of all. They really need help, not only in academics but "life." This is the first summer they have ever had a counselor, and I am pretty proud of the way it came about. I got the university to give us a grant for the program to provide counseling for these children through the summer and I in return would not only

act as the counselor but coordinate graduate student volunteers from the university who want to work with children. Everyone benefits and I am even getting a small stipend. I am excited about the program and will tell you all about it when it starts in July.

George is coming down here for a visit June 19th, and he and his wife move to Gainesville August 15th. They are still excited about the move and their first baby, which is due October 16th.

Our daughter, Kate, has lost eighty-five pounds and still trying to lose sixty more. She has always had an extreme weight problem and finally decided to take action. She had gastroplasty, where they staple the stomach, and has no complications from her surgery. It was a drastic measure but necessary for her health and self-esteem. I am so proud of her.

All the dogs are shedding their winter coats all over us and the house. We do plan to get another puppy this summer for breeding, and anyone who knows us says that we are crazy to have six dogs. Oh well!!! Emmy, the cat, is especially dismayed.

Chris sends his best. He will be finishing up his internship to become a principal this summer and will teach in the classroom at least another year.... I think about you and pray for you every day. Lots of love, Janet"

* * *

My mother, my older brother, and his wife were now living in the Turks and Caicos Islands. They had purchased fifty acres to develop into a tourist resort and were quite busy making that happen. After building a house for my mother, they constructed five cottages to rent, and my brother became a general contractor overseeing lot purchase and construction of individual homes for investors. The purchasers only spend a limited amount of time each year in their homes. That led to my mother and brother becoming landlords in charge of leasing individual vacation homes. It was a full-time job, and I had little contact with any of them. More about the islands later.

* * *

The facts are not pretty. I have been hospitalized six times, and there has been little communication with any of my family. I know that my father is quite ill, which means I have no parents that give a shit. I am trying to take responsibility for my life, but it is so difficult reaching the grown-up status. I expect my parents to take care of me, to love me unconditionally. Why I hang on to this myth, I would eventually understand.

June 17, 1998
"Dear Admiral… It is that time of year again when fathers everywhere are honored, and I want you to be no exception. You and I certainly have an unusual father–daughter relationship, but I am just thankful that we have had one at all. My trip to Florida with George, was the best and even though it was a short lunch, it was the best lunch that I had with my father. George told me how neat it was to meet his grandfather.
I thought that I would have time to go visit Mother in the Turks and Caicos this August, but there is just not enough time and it is not going to happen. Maybe she will come to the States in the fall.
Please drop us a line if you get the chance and have an absolutely wonderful Father's Day!!! Love, Janet"

June 17, 1998

"Dear Janet… Thanks for the greeting and the message. It is tough going and no assurance of any success. It is not if I am going to die now; it is when. I will keep you advised better. Matt"

There was no question that the Admiral was declining, and it would be six months before I heard from him again. Silence is not always golden. I was getting older, and my father was dying. I did hope that we would see each other again, but I was convinced that was not going to happen.

December 22, 1998

"Dear Janet… I have no idea how to get you on the net at this point so here goes a letter to you. Things are pretty depressing at this time with my wife gone, but the children are taking good care of me. Hope you gave had a nice holiday and will have happy and healthy New Year. My outlook is not very promising but then I have had a full life and have no regrets and all of us most (sic) go sometime. I will keep in touch with you. Best to the family. Love Matt"

February 27, 1999

"Dear Dad… I desperately need a dad right now! I don't know if you are still online but please answer this if you are. We are having serious problems and I need your experience and your wisdom. I love you, Janet"

March 2, 1999

"Dear Dad… I need a dad right now. Since the beginning of this year, Chris and I have had so many challenges that I feel I'm losing the race even though I can't walk. I have had back problems since last May and was finally operated on February 8 in Charlottesville at the University Hospital. Scar tissue and a disk were removed. There was major improvement, but I have a great deal of pain in my left leg and back. One week after surgery we drove to Akron for Chris's dad's funeral. That was extremely painful just riding in the car and I was an emotional wreck at the funeral. One week after we returned home (last Friday), I was fired from my school counseling job. The county was very careful legally not to imply that I was let go because of being out so long, so they used poor performance as the reason. Last year and every evaluation before that showed exemplary work, dedication to the school and negated everything that this evaluation said. We just don't have the resources or money to fight it. I will probably have to go back on disability until I can be trained for my next career. Whatever that might be....

I need to end this because I am in a very bad mood and it is not right to dump all this stuff on you. I hope you are alright. I want to see you again when I am in Gainesville visiting George, or I want to be notified immediately of your death. Either way I want the opportunity to say goodbye. I love you and I need to do that. It sounds kind of depressive, but it is reality and part of life. I love you very much and am very proud of you, Janet"

I wanted to touch him again, to be embraced by him, and to see his soft smile. I knew this was the end and felt so powerless and helpless. My sponsor had instilled a mantra in my mind throughout the years in recovery. That is what I thought of. "God's in charge." It was short and yet so comforting. My life was so busy that I just put my father on a shelf and tried to forget that he was dying.

At the same time, I was being fired from my job, and it was really a big deal. It did result from hospitalization and an ill-informed superintendent. My contract was not renewed, and the only reason was my disclosure of being a person with bipolar disorder. I could have invoked my rights under the American Disabilities Act and made a stink of the whole ordeal. Stigma was alive and well. Truthfully, I was ready to make a move and resigned peacefully. I had a considerable resentment and needed to resolve that ongoing rage toward my principal. I was tired, drained. My feelings of wanting to retaliate or get even did not disturb anyone but me.

They say that God does not shut one door without opening another. I felt like all the doors, and the windows, were sealed shut, and I needed a giant crowbar to get out. Being unemployed or maybe unemployable hit me full force this time. I was carrying so much guilt about my son, David, that it was hard to focus on a new direction.

Years later, this man walked up to me during a local street fair and gave me a big hug. Once I recognized that he was my former principal, the gregarious greeting made no sense. However, I realized that I had forgiven him, and the resentment was gone.

* * *

Late April of 1999, I did not realize that I was experiencing a full-blown manic attack. The signs were there, but I did not see them. I was juggling so many balls that one was bound to fall. There is one guarantee when you are riding a manic high. You will crash into depression, and the higher you are, the further you will fall. I was hospitalized experiencing a full psychotic break and could not see any way out except for suicide. My best plans did not work, but I came awfully close. I hung myself in my hospital room. There was a dividing curtain between the two beds in my room. They had not taken my bra away from me upon admittance. I carefully tied my bra around my neck, stood on the night table, fastened the other end around the curtain and jumped off the table. I was full of equal parts of fear, guilt, and excitement. I do not know how long I hung there, but that nurse jumped on me to bring me down. I started sobbing and was totally uncontrollable. My psychiatrist was called, and I was given strong sedatives to calm down. They put me in the quiet room in four-point restraints. Everyone said that it was for my own safety. My tears were a long time coming, and every drop was for David. Finally, the dam had broken, and all the hurt, the guilt, the remorse came flooding out. Little did I know that that would be the turning point in my life. I did not need a parent, a mother, a father, a husband, or a child to fix me. I wanted to start living again. I really did want to fly. I felt like circumstances, not a bulldozer, like the Dr. Seuss story, had gently put me back in the nest. I felt safe and confident that I could handle life on life's terms. It had been almost five years since David died.

Chapter 7: Letting Go

I was asked recently by a young woman living with bipolar disorder, "At what age did you finally accept your disease?" Wow! I had to really think about that and finally confessed to her that it was in my late forties when I was in a psychiatric hospital and accepted that my son had died, and no one was to blame. "I think that I accepted my disease when I surrendered and let go of all the anger." She thanked me for sharing my experience and made an incredible comment, "I want to grow up to be just like you. I want to have balance in my life and learn to live with this illness." We left it at that, but it was an eye-opener as to how far I had come. My life journey not only had detours but new signs along the way. I was learning to STOP, YIELD, and PROCEED WITH CAUTION.

April 9, 1999
"Hi Janet... This is Patricia, the Admiral's granddaughter. He is doing okay, but does not get on his computer much anymore, so I print his email for him. I will see him tomorrow so I will give him this message. Maybe you can call him at (904) 246-2261. Thanks."

* * *

May 23, 1999, my mother telephoned to tell me that the Admiral, my father, had died. I do not know how she got that information, but

I was thankful to get the call. It was ironic that she was the one to deliver the message. Chris had a couple of Navy friends, and he got the details of the funeral.

Chapter 8: The Secret Is Out

We have come full circle in my memoir. You have already heard how I felt at that military funeral service in Arlington, Virginia. It was the beginning of my story, but not the end. I felt so left out. I knew what it was like to feel like a square peg in a round circle. It had been several years since I had seen my father, and I thought that it was time to break the code of secrecy. After the funeral service, Chris and I did attend the reception. We did not get an invitation, because no one in the Admiral's family knew that I existed. A significant change in my life was about to take place.

* * *

Since the age of nineteen, I had kept that special red notebook of every letter that my father had ever written and a few mementos from our visits. It was that three-ring binder that I took to the reception. I did not really have a plan. With Chris at my side for moral support, I approached the Admiral's only son, Jim, and asked him for a few minutes of his time. Not knowing what to expect, he led us over to a private corner of the room, and we all stood silent for that exceptionally long minute where time hangs in the air. Finally, I held up the notebook and realized that it was not going to speak. It was time for me to get some courage. I felt like I blurted out, "You are my brother, Jim. The Admiral is my father. I mean Matt was my father." Jim had a perplexed look, and I really did not know where to go from there. I held up the notebook and showed him the first letter that was signed "Dad." I told him that I had known for thirty years but was asked to keep secret this relationship as no one in his family knew of his "indiscretion." That word was another euphemism that turned my stomach. The Admiral slept with my mother one night, and I was the result. I had heard the phrase bastard before and refused to go that far. I was a mistake, but as the Admiral had told me, a good mistake and not a loser.

The funeral reception opened up an entirely new world and included my one half brother and four half sisters. Jim did not seem that surprised and immediately called over to his sisters to join us in a small anteroom off the central reception area. Jim announced my news to his siblings. There were four entirely different reactions, and I stood my ground. Jim showed his sisters the notebook, and I remained silent until I heard the response from my new oldest half sister. "Thank God my mother is not here, and she passed before you came forward." Now I know what it is like to be "outed," to come out of the closet, to disclose your true identity. It had taken forty-nine years, but the family secret had been blown. I did ask if I could contact Jim and the sisters individually. Carol, the oldest, answered for everyone, "What do you want from us?" I had expected this response and had a reply. "I do not want money. I just wanted to meet my brother and sisters." When I answered Carol's question, I knew I wanted more than any of them could give me. I wanted my father that we had just buried. There was no doubt that he was my father in my mind, but I could see all the denial and disbelief in this new-found family. They were looking at me like I had horns growing out of my head and huge extended hands asking for handouts. Everyone looked at the notebook and seemed cautiously impressed with the "Love, Dad" letter. There was that awkward silence again that filled at least three more minutes and felt like twenty. Jim took over and suggested we exchange home addresses and contact each other in the future. "Future" was an odd word. Did he mean this week, this month, or next year? It turned out that each sister and Jim had their own interpretation of time.

The year following the funeral, we did get a surprise visit from Jim and his son, Parker. We spent a couple of days together, visiting the university, hiking up our local waterfalls, going for a drive up to Mountain Lake, and talking, lots of talking. The visit was fantastic, and I was excited to discover my new brother and nephew. To this day, I do not know what happened. Jim moved to Seattle, and all communication stopped. I did get an email during the Christmas holidays and a couple of messages on Facebook, but that was it. I just assumed that something had been said during his visit that was offensive, fearful, or pushed the wrong buttons. After trying to reach Jim for a couple of years, I gave up and waited to hear from him. I feared that he had found out that I had a serious mental illness and he no longer wanted a relationship. By this time, I was not keeping my bipolar disorder a family secret. This conclusion as to why Jim was cutting me out of his life was probably farfetched, but it had occurred with a past friend, so it was not entirely unfounded. In any case, my priorities had definitely changed, and the "father" issue was on hold. I was spending more time with my immediate family.

Chapter 9: My Nest

I am going to backtrack and look at my new unemployment. There is a difference in being unemployed and unemployable. Having resigned as a school counselor, the school system was no longer an option. I was headed in a new direction. It was time to take a breather and figure out what I was going to do with the rest of life. Fortunately, I still had the excellent support team that was helping me stay sober. My husband, my daughter, my son, my psychiatrist, my counselor, and my sponsor were my management team. It would take each one of them to help me be an active member of my family, my community, and learn how to love myself. The last goal was the toughest. Building my confidence, increasing my self-esteem, and learning to fly solo was a tall, tall order. It was not an event that happened one weekend. My sponsor told me it was like peeling an onion, and each layer would uncover who I was and who I wanted to be. It was a process and did require constant vigilance. There were sad days. I no longer said things like, "If only I had a father to hold my hand. If only I had a father to …." I had grown past that excuse. His death and his funeral were behind me. It was time to move on, as they say. Who would be a part of this new journey, and did I have a firm reliance on those around me? Some days yes, and some days no. Once you have decided to live, connections and relationships are possible. It is possible to mature like a ripe green apple that turns red. I was positively green, a newcomer to this line of thinking. What was important to me and what were my priorities?

My sponsor in recovery told me that I overthought everything. It was a way that I could control or think that I managed what was happening around the people who lived in my world and me. She was right. There was that illusion, and it was hard to let go and just trust. Faith is believing what you cannot see. I had no church home, and my faith was shaky on a regular basis. How did all that play out?

* * *

It is time for a little introspection. During the search for my father-daughter relationship, there was a dual track happening in my life. My children were spreading their wings and creating experiences of their own. Recapping their movements after high school will help clarify where my kids were during the dark days and afterward in recovery.

My daughter graduated from high school the same year that our son, David, died, and I remember so little about her graduation. Maybe the ECT took a higher toll than I thought. For whatever reason, those memories are blocked or missing forever.

Kate moved out of our house when she turned eighteen and enrolled in the local university. We were estranged in so many ways, and I wanted her back. I do not know how she felt during that time of transition, but I felt abandoned. That was a feeling that I knew very well through all my years growing up and into adulthood. It reared its ugly head and simmered over the next few years. Somehow I had that stinkin' thinkin' that the world continued to revolve around me, and I was being hurt by my daughter and my son by their absence. I do understand that many parents encounter the empty nest syndrome and feel depressed when their kids go out into the world. Since my moods tend to go to the extreme, there was an overwhelming sense of loss. It was time to let go. Maybe I missed the drama and needed to accept once again that life goes on, circumstances create change, and situations evolve that give us the opportunity for growth. Having said all that, I was so sad to see my daughter, Kate, get her own apartment with four of her high school buddies and not be at the breakfast table. I helped her set up her house, bought her a Mr. Coffee, and visited the retail store where she worked at least once a week.

My oldest son graduated from high school in 1991 and continued his academic studies in Boulder, Colorado, where he met the girl that he was going to marry. They both transferred to Indiana University to save some money and ended up at the University of New Mexico in El Paso, closer to his fiancée's family home in Texas. Getting married on a ranch was their decision and was extremely exciting for our family, all but George's father. He had quite a few words of discontent and was totally ignored. It was the beginning of the end of that father–son relationship. George and his new wife moved to Florida for graduate school, where he had met the Admiral, his grandfather. It had been four years since David's death.

The same year we had an incredible call from our oldest son. "Mom, you are now a grandma." It was exciting news, and I could not wait to head south and visit our new grandson, Kevin. That first visit was magical. He looked just like his father when he was born. George weighed eight pounds and fourteen ounces at birth, and his new son was also a big baby and a bright-eyed toe-head. My only disappointment was that they lived so far away. I did manage several visits and watched him grow into a highly active toddler. About that time, George asked if we could bring them a puppy. Since our son was in graduate school studying biology, chemistry, and physics, it was not a surprise that the puppy was named Photon (a particle of light). Kevin and Photon became best buds, and we had no idea where that would go.

The following year during Christmas, George, his wife, and Kevin, came to visit. The weather was unusually warm on the farm, and George asked if we could go for a walk. I was excited by the invitation and put on my muckrakers to walk around the pasture with the goats. George does not mince words. "I have decided to get a divorce." "What?" I was not prepared for that announcement, and it was going to upset my Norman Rockwell Christmas. My husband and I loved his wife, our daughter-in-law, and rated their marriage as a 10. However, this was not about us. Living out of state, George was more distant than our daughter, but I thought that I had a good pulse on his marital life. Wrong. The reasons for the separation were not significant as the acceptance that his family was breaking up. We were still wandering around the pasture and turned to head home. The Christmas week and the few family traditions that we maintained continued with the elephant in the middle of the room. I spent as much time as possible with my grandson and held him just a little bit tighter than previous visits.

Being a grandmother is more comfortable for me than being a mother. I had an excellent mentor, Grandma Lee. She even looked like a grandma. Gray hair that sparkled in the sunshine and round glasses that lit up her eyes are the two images that always come to mind. She was short, the shortest one in the family, and kind of plump, but not fat. I still cannot figure how her nurturing, caring, loving personality skipped my mother's generation big time. Grandma Lee was my rock in a totally dysfunctional family. At age five, I went to spend two weeks with Grandma in Iowa. It is perplexing how I cannot remember what happened five years ago, but I can recall that summer in the country. We spent most of the vacation netting butterflies and pressing them into the World Book Encyclopedia, Volume J for Janet. Environmentalists and "Save the Butterfly" groups would not have approved, but that just never came up. I sat on my grandma's lap on her front step. She would give me big hugs and tell me how beautiful I was. There was a grandpa, but he just stayed to himself. Grandma Lee would spend hours (probably minutes) brushing my hair and putting bright ribbons on top to hold back my bangs. I remember these things, or I have seen the photos and perceive these moments. It does not really matter. Grandma Lee continued to be a safe haven in a storm. Through the years she would visit my mother and share her love with all of us. I am fairly sure Grandma preferred granddaughters over grandsons because my younger sister, Lynn, got the same special treatment as I remember. I never asked my mother why she could not be more like her mother, but I sure thought it. It would take my mother seventy more years to say "I love you."

Chapter 10: I Am Responsible

Parenting is a big topic. There are hundreds, if not thousands, of books on that subject and I have read quite a few. It just seems that parenting skills and behaviors are passed from one generation to the next. *God, I love my kids, but how do I raise them?*

There was unfortunately not a nurturing gene in my mother, and she spent most of her life trying to avoid mothering. I knew that she was not a great role model, and I am so thankful that I had Grandma Lee and my childhood family, the Pierces, to emulate. The week that my grandmother died, I was able to talk to her on the phone and tell her that my life had turned around. I was sober and in a recovery program. I told her how much I loved her, and she said, "I love you too, and you make me so very happy." What a beautiful gift she gave me, and it would last a lifetime.

***

What about my children? There were many parenting skills that I learned the hard way. An event would take place and we could accept it or we could not accept it. There were no other options. George not only got a divorce that year, but he announced a new wife from Serbia. He had graduated from his doctoral program in Florida, and he was going to move to California for a postdoctoral program at Stanford. We were asked to come pick up Photon, since it was impossible to find housing in Palo Alto for a huge yellow Labrador Retriever. Oh, by the way, Photon had been taught only Serbian commands and did not speak English anymore. That was a challenge. Do we continue his Serbian and teach our eight other Labs a new language? Absolutely not. We picked up Photon and said our goodbyes. I feared that I had lost my grandson after the divorce, and now my son was moving 2,700 miles away from me.

* * *

About that time, I discovered a huge resentment from working the 12 Steps that AA suggests. It is a procedure that allows you to visit your past, make amends for any wrongdoing, and identify those persons that you feel have negatively affected you. I had a great deal of anger directed at my ex-husband, who I felt had not only harmed me but also hurt David inconsolably. My middle son had lived with his father in Colorado from the time he was ten years old until he graduated from high school. After graduation he was told to go to college or whatever, but he must make his own way in life at eighteen years of age. That is when David caught up with his older brother and followed George to Las Cruces, New Mexico. As mentioned earlier, I do not think David ever committed to a college or one area of interest, other than disk golf. After all, he was my free-spirited, artistic, creative boy of few words. That is where the resentment unfolded. After David's death, I blamed his father for the tragedy and maintained if David had not been kicked out of his house at eighteen, maybe he would have not dropped out of college, gone to Mexico, or died at such a young age. That "what if" reasoning was not helping my emotional sobriety and it was time to let go of the huge resentment. It did not happen overnight.

After years of learning how to let go and practicing rational reasoning, I have successfully forgiven Wes and learned to "move on."

There are many early years in David's life that I cannot recall and periods of his childhood living with his father that I was not privy to. Accepting the memories that I have and sharing David's story as mine unfolds is a gift that keeps on giving.

* * *

When I was attempting to raise my three children, it did occur to me that despite my criticism of my parents, adoptive or biological, there was one fact that I could not deny. All had left me a vibrant legacy that included words, deeds, and character. In some cases, I learned what not to do. But there were some lessons that I was taught which would benefit me for my lifetime.

* * *

My mother, Dottie Marie, was the most dynamic and strongest woman I have ever met. She did not lift weights or bench 200 pounds. Her strengths were her persistence and incredible ability to think creatively. During dark periods when her dreams slipped away, she stood taller, worked harder, and pushed her way to success in the business world. What about the private sector, her family? It took years of experience, but I now know how difficult it is to live with an alcoholic, bury one, and not let addictions ruin your life. My mother was the best enabler ever. And yet, she survived without being sucked into the disease of alcoholism. Living with my stepfather had to be sheer hell. The confusion, the disappointments, the constant crisis usually destroys the alcoholic's significant other. It just caused my mother to work smarter, to hold things together, and to be persistent in her own goals. The critical objective for my mother during my early years was to make money, lots of money. If that meant standing tall and supporting her husband at his worst, she was in for the long hall. The development and construction business thrived, and my mother should take all the credit. She gave me her tenacity and her business acuity that would show up in my future careers.

What about the alcoholic? What did Al Williams, my stepfather, give me as his legacy? For years I blamed him for my alcoholism. After all, we know there is a genetic, familial connection in the disease. There was one big problem. I did not have his genes and was not remotely related to him. It was time to let him off the hook for that one. However, being an alcoholic is not easy either. He was a brilliant man, obviously loved my mother, and just could not stop drinking. God knows that he tried. Alcoholism did not kill him, but it would have eventually. The brain tumor that took his life was insidious, and he survived two brain surgeries to cut it out. He lived three years when the medical professionals gave him two months. Al Williams's middle name was "persistence." He seemed bigger than life sometimes. He actually was, big that is. He stood tall at six feet four inches with broad shoulders and a long gait. Whenever I tried to keep up with him while walking the beach, I had to speed walk just to stay close. I think that he loved me, at least sometimes. He had deep-blue piercing eyes and an enormous belly laugh. It came from deep inside his stomach and lasted an exceptionally long time. I think that I heard him laugh about once a week. I never kept track, but I remember him coming home early almost every Friday. He was usually in a good mood, and that is when he would laugh at something, anything. What did I learn from my stepfather? Once I accepted that I was an alcoholic, I remembered his fight and how he lost. If he could not stop drinking, why would I be able to do that? The legacy that I received was a gift of knowledge and experience from one alcoholic to another. I needed help to live my life sober and would never make it alone.

* * *

Where does character come from? That is a loaded question that has baffled philosophers, scientists, and psychiatrists alike. How much is nature and how much is nurture? It has always been interesting to me that I do not question my light switch on the wall. I do not ponder and spend endless nights asking how electricity works. Radio waves are another common occurrence that leave me speechless. Cell phones? You have the idea. My disposition and my personality do come from somewhere or someone. Who did pass on these glaring traits? Let's look at the bad stuff first.

Self-righteous anger, free-floating fear, outright stubbornness, inability to always be truthful, and extremely poor self-esteem make up the list that you will see in my therapist's file folder. I have addressed each of these with several sponsors and counselors over the years and have unsuccessfully blamed my parents for passing on to me these character defects. My conclusion is that I am human and not incredibly unique. In other words, these are emotions that all of us possess, and we work hard not to let them overrun our lives. All the intangible feelings that rule our behavior are who we are. I am no exception.

Fortunately, there are positive emotions too. Persistence, courage, compassion, and creativity, to name a few. The battle begins. Yes, my bipolar disorder and my alcoholism add another ingredient to the equation. I have come to realize that my mother, my stepfather, my biological father, and my grandmother left me a legacy that helped to shape who I am becoming. The roads to life, the journey, not the destination, give me direction. Life is not a race. People who are part of this life adventure contribute immensely to my character, good and bad. My job is to grow spiritually and ethically to be the best person that I can be. I have all this insight and what do I do with it?

Chapter 11: Learning to Soar

Back to the farm and present day. Our daughter is married, has one beautiful red-headed son, and lives less than twenty minutes up the road, or up the road "a piece" as they say here in our county. Kate entered the computer software industry and quickly moved up the ladder to be a successful sales manager and vice president. She is married to a terrific man, husband, and father. Having my daughter and my daughter's family close in proximity is especially important to me as I watch her walk through her own roads of life and can share her experiences. Having my youngest grandson for weekly visits, watching his baseball games, and fielding his constant why, how, when questions are such a blessing.

George is now living in California. After trying to make a failing marriage work, he moved to Texas to be near his two sons, Brad and Bobbie, and met the love of his life. They were married last February and moved to San Francisco to pursue excellent job opportunities. My son is incredibly innovative and is in the process of starting up his own research company. He and his new wife recently celebrated the birth of their child, Sophie, my first granddaughter.

Chris is retired from teaching school and spends a great deal of time taking our certified therapy dogs to visit different facilities. Delivering their unconditional love is extremely rewarding to him, and I am enormously proud of all that he does to help others.

I am a retired licensed professional counselor. The transition from the school system to a licensed therapist was not smooth but most rewarding. That journey needs to be shared.

* * *

When I was a school counselor, there was an underlying frustration that made the job ineffective. Serving as the sole guidance counselor in an elementary school with 420 students, it was impossible to address all the needs and wants. When there was a crisis, parents were often a part of the problem but rarely a part of the solution. Excellent teachers and devoted staff could not always fix what was broken. As the school counselor, I often felt like I was putting a Band-Aid on a problem that needed major surgery. Family counseling, engaging the entire family would be so much more effective, but rarely occurred. I wanted to learn more, to experience more, and to help more. Fourteen challenging courses, an internship, and a state exam were required to move into this new direction. I completed the coursework, landed an internship in the local community services organization, and just needed to pass the licensing test to become a licensed professional counselor. Sometimes it feels like you are jumping over the hurdles and hitting a brick wall, or there is just not enough Kleenex.

* * *

How can one person's nose run continuously and her eyes flow like a faucet? I had no cold, no allergies that I knew of, and had never heard of this phenomenon as a reaction to stress.

Here I sat with a small Kleenex packet and no explanation for what was happening to me. There were twenty people in the room lined up, one behind the other, in medium-sized student desks in four rows. Someone must have marked where each chair should be placed because it seemed too perfect as to how the chairs were all facing the test proctor in the front of the room. It reminded me of cadets at a memorial service in perfect formation standing silently waiting for their commander's next order. However, this was not a funeral, it just felt that way.

This was one of the most important tests in my life. It was going to determine my second career. I had already completed sixteen graduate courses, but this was the big hurdle. Unless I passed this exam, I would not be a mental health professional, be licensed, or be able to practice as a therapist. In other words, I had to pass this test.

The morning had been uneventful. The alarm sounded at six and I jumped out of bed ready for battle. I had laid out my clothes the night before and deliberately chosen an outfit that was suited for test taking. You know, loose and comfortable. I had the breakfast of champions, just like the cereal box advertised and enough coffee to alert my brain. The drive to the test site was about an hour, and I left enough time to drive there twice. Halfway on route, my eyes started doing funny things. They started weeping. I was extremely anxious so maybe that was the cause of this involuntary crying. Fortunately, I was prepared and had thrown a small packet of Kleenex in my purse. I arrived at the test site very early (on purpose) so I could find the best seat, near the front, and locate the ladies' room. *Semper Paratus*!

By the time the proctor started giving us directions, at 8 am on the dot, my nose was beginning to run continuously and both eyes required wiping every few minutes. What was going on? I was already halfway through my tissues, and my pencil had not touched the examination. This was a timed test and we were told that we had exactly two hours to complete and not one minute more. During that time, I was going to regurgitate all the course material that I had completed, facts and figures from the cram course that I took twice, and information that my creative mind was supposed to reconfigure for the test.

Since we had to get permission to leave the room, use the facilities, or get a drink of water, I managed ten minutes of filling in little circles with my pencil before I had to leave and collect toilet paper, to stop the deluge. I kept running low on my supply and had to replenish with a trip to the bathroom. Running out of Kleenex was not on the list of excusable pauses in test-taking. Too bad!

It was after the third exit that I knew I was in trouble. I could not see. My eyesight was clouded with tears that were the size of humongous drops of rain, and there was no stopping this waterfall. I just plowed through the test in silent prayer that it would soon be over. I did not finish the test when I heard, "Put your pencils down!"

Two weeks have passed, and I check the mailbox every day for my test results. Finally, the envelope arrives, and I see the results in black and white. It is a very short letter suggesting that I retest. I failed by two points.

Let's go back to that fateful day. When I arrived home, my husband took one look and drove me the emergency room. Somehow, someway, I had gotten a piece of plastic in my left eye, and that was the culprit that foretold my fate of retesting and trying again. So much for failure!

Today I am a practicing mental health professional and only recount this story when people ask, "Was the licensed counselor's exam difficult?" There is usually a pause on my part before I respond, "Not the second time."

My internship began in January of 2000, a new century, and a new beginning. I was now a licensed professional counselor and had a paper from the state to prove it. Part of the licensing process was to complete a one-semester internship in the counseling field. I interviewed with the local Community Service Board and got lucky, incredibly lucky. My new supervisor assigned me to work with the substance abuse program, called Stepping Stones, and she had no idea that I was in recovery. Six weeks into the internship, I was offered a full-time paid position with benefits. It would be my last full-time job ever.

Working with alcoholics and drug addicts is an incredible challenge. It is the only disease that tells you that you don't have it. So, why seek treatment? The denial builds a considerable stone wall around the addicted person and waves a flag stating, "Leave me alone. I'm fine." That is why it is absolutely necessary that the addict hit bottom, a place where the only choice is to get help or die. Most, but not all, the men and women in Stepping Stones had used up all their excuses, run out of people to blame, and were physically and mentally bankrupt. We had their attention, and most were ready to lay down the gauntlet and follow a new life plan. Group counseling, twelve-step meetings three times a week, and turn your whole life around was the prescription. It was a pretty simple program for complicated people, but not an easy one. The success rate was poor and has not gotten much better over the years.

The first six months of this paid internship was brutal. Not only did I facilitate the recovery program, but I was also expected to carry a full client load. Scheduling clients, seeing clients, and referring individual clients is a full-time job without the substance abuse groups. Something had to give. I was managing my bipolar disorder and my own sobriety with my excellent support network. My spiritual program was not great but progressing.

At the end of my third year, the dam broke. I was physically exhausted and did not know it. I was not taking time out for me, and it showed. I was not directly lying to anyone; I just was not talking and was again lying by omission. About this time, one of my clients committed suicide. I had seen him late that evening, and it was our last visit. Memories of all my own previous suicide attempts came flooding back, and I realized that I was in trouble. Denial had grabbed hold of me, and I admitted to myself that I had been thinking suicidally for months. Just like many of my clients, I saw no other way out. There was only one safe place for me to go. Chris drove me to the psychiatric hospital, and the ECT treatments began again. I resigned reluctantly from my counseling position and was once again unemployed.

* * *

I am sitting in a waiting room analyzing the recent course of events. Fear, confusion, and a little self-loathing seem to be present. "How did I end up here?" My husband and I are in Baltimore, Maryland, waiting for an appointment with Dr. Grover. The purpose of this visit is to get a collaborative diagnosis of my psychiatric illness and check my cognitive functioning. I am back at John Hopkins. This is where you go when you hit a brick wall, and you don't know where else to go. My skin feels all tingly and I keep having these waves of nausea. The visit is the second referral to this hospital from my psychiatrist back home. He was a bit surprised by my last psychotic breakdown and wants collaboration on the best course of treatment to follow. In other words, even though I am medication compliant, have all the textbook symptoms of bipolar disorder, and have not missed one ECT appointment, my course of treatment is being questioned. They do not know what to do with me. More important, is what they are doing to me bad for me?

For the next three days at the hospital, I talked to various therapists, worked every kind of puzzle, and took every memory recall test known to Freud and others. When you see that you know the answer and it will not emerge, it is a bit like being constipated. It is there, but it won't come out. I felt incredibly frustrated and doubted my own abilities to spell my name right. The results, once again, confirmed the bipolar diagnosis with alcoholism and drug addiction. Duh! The recommendation was to continue therapy, counseling, twelve-step recovery, and to have ECT once a month as a maintenance function. It was suggested that I continue working, but only part-time, get lots of rest, and return to John Hopkins in eighteen months, not a year or two, but just in one year and a half. It took three years to return, and a lot happened in the interim. Let's fill in some of the gaps.

***

This entire story has a focus on my father, and we know that he is dead and buried. What about my mother whom I described earlier? Sticking to her hope for a geographic cure, she has now moved from California to the Turks and Caicos Islands. Her latest male companion died in Santa Barbara. He was probably the best catch yet and was indeed a wonderful man. Why go halfway around the world to a deserted island?

It has finally occurred to me that my mother is probably living with an undiagnosed bipolar disorder. During her manic phases, she moves locations. The depression is well-disguised as she isolates and just does not talk to anyone. I could add a few more clinical labels, but telling her story reveals most of her personality quirks. There would be some controversy among family members in describing her character defects. It is at your discretion as to the glaring descriptors you might use. My mother is incredibly narcissistic, and we'll leave it at that.

***

What about my older brother, Edward? He had been living in California. He was an engineer, designing miniature submarines, and was thinking of changing jobs. We never saw each other, and I did not believe he and my mother were frequent visitors. It was a surprise when I got that call that they were all leaving California and were moving to the British West Indies to develop a fifty-acre piece of raw land into a resort. What? Under further review, I found out that the island was called Middle Caicos in the Turks and Caicos and had fewer than hundred people in residence. Half of them were children, and most originated from Haiti. It was a poorly developed place that did have a couple churches, a one-room school, a visiting magistrate, and gorgeous white-sand beaches. At first, I was kind of jealous. It sounded like Gilligan's Island. I guess the millionaire was my mother. The professor was my brother, Edward, and his wife, Terri, was the movie star. Except, this was not a reality show, and the characters were my family. It would be years before I visited this motley crew on their deserted island.

***

Back in the old USA, golf was taking priority in my life. I had gotten hooked about twenty years earlier but had to stop due to lupus. It is a funny thing about autoimmune diseases. If you live long enough, the affliction will either kill you or you will go into remission. I am one of the lucky ones, the symptoms started subsiding. I got back to golf with a vengeance. After joining my county golf club and buying a cart, the only thing that I needed was to play. I was currently unemployed, so time was not an issue. My golfing adventures took me within a thirty-mile radius around my house and eventually, I headed to Florida to visit my original golf mentor, Joan. My treks to Florida were special because of Joan and Linda, my first AA sponsor. Staying with these two women for one week every year was my annual spiritual retreat. They had known me at my worst and still loved me. There were never any masks that I needed to hide behind, and I could just be me. What an arrangement! What a gift! Linda liked to shop and cook. After a round of golf, Joan and I would come home to a wonderful, sumptuous meal. Occasionally, the evening would include a game of Poker, Phase 10, Skip Bo or we would go to a twelve-step meeting. For a nightcap, we all enjoyed our favorite coffee ice cream complete with chocolate syrup and whipped cream. If I close my eyes, I can taste that sweet, succulent dessert.

We would play golf every day possible, and then I would reluctantly catch the budget airline special to home. It was basking on one of those spectacular courses in Florida, waiting to putt, that I got the call that would send me in a different direction. I usually do not carry a cell phone when golfing, let alone answer it. Maybe God was doing his anonymous thing again. For whatever reason, I sauntered over to my cart and picked up the call.

***

It seems that being unemployed had made me available for an exciting new project. This woman calls and in the middle of my golf game asks if I had heard anything about pre-bond or post-bond treatment programs. She got my attention and asked if I would fly home to talk to the powers-to-be about a newly funded grant that needed my participation. My flight home was bumped up a couple of days, and the interviews began. Our federal government had found some monies to treat recovering alcoholics and/or addicts who had a comorbid diagnosis of mental illness. The details are a bit cumbersome, but the gist of the idea is simple. Judges have the option of assigning a perpetrator to a one-year treatment program instead of jail. The treatment plan is extensive. One screwup by the accused, and they go to prison without passing go. I was hired to plan the training for this bunch and to oversee a group of peers, who were already in recovery, to act as mentors. The team needed my personal experience with a mental illness and my expertise as a substance abuse counselor. Two problems existed: first, I was on disability, and second, I was told not to work full-time. My new boss had a solution for both. Decide how many hours I want to work and tell them how much money I want to make without affecting my disability income. In other words, I could write my own ticket and be hired because I had a mental illness and was in recovery. It was nice to be wanted, and I had no idea what I really was going to be doing. Life-changing events were about to happen.

Before the new work schedule kicked in, my counselor and psychiatrist suggested another trip to Johns Hopkins Psychiatric Hospital in Baltimore. My mood had been stabilized, but my memory was feeble. Did I have cognitive damage from all the ECTs and should they be continued? The answer was yes and yes. No one would say what might have caused a slight cognitive impairment, but the memory deficit was another story. If my husband and I went to a movie on Friday, I would recall the title the following Monday but not the storyline, the plot, or any of the actors. All that information is somewhat superfluous and not of significant concern; but remembering names, events, and dates is significant. The consultation at John Hopkins summarized some actions steps that I needed to take. First, as previously recommended, continue the maintenance ECT once a month. My reaction to that suggestion was a disappointment. Taking one day a month, driving to the next state, receiving general anesthesia, suffering from a severe headache, recovering for the next two days, and remembering less was not the treatment plan that I would have selected. It is scary. ECT was another family secret, and I had already had enough secrets for a lifetime.

I started going for treatments in a hospital, three hours from my home to avoid running into clients or other pillars of the community. It did occur to me if I ran into a person I knew having ECT, they would be just as embarrassed, feel just as stigmatized, and feel just as judged as I did. I opted to go out of town for treatments. This decision helped me to stand up to my whole support team and tell them in 2007 that I was done with ECT. I was not going to go for any more treatments, and everyone would just have to back off and see the results.

Now, we are ready to start the new job. The life-changing event came outside of the work parameter and was part of a volunteer position that I accepted at the same time. Across the country, beginning in Memphis, Tennessee, the Crisis Intervention Team training was spreading. Law enforcement, dispatchers, firemen, and other first responders were learning what to do if the call involved someone with a mental illness. Taking them to the ER, locking someone up in jail, or taking them to a shelter was very ineffective. It was time to teach this helping population how to help. I was asked to participate by attending the training in Memphis and speaking to each new class from the perspective of the mentally ill person. Standing in front of policemen, detectives, and others who might interact with the mentally ill population was a colossal undertaking. For the first time, I was "outing" myself in my community, taking off all my masks, and telling this group what it was really like. The stigma, the confusion, the misdiagnosing, and the poor treatment of those with severe mental illness were about to improve. The first time that I spoke, the room was packed, and my anxiety was building. Since I do not perspire, I have another skin sensation which I experienced at Johns Hopkins and is equally terrifying—my skin tingles. There is a slight tremor, but nothing that anyone else would notice. I heard my name, and I was being introduced to the crowd.

Thirty to forty-five minutes seemed like a lifetime until I got up to speak. It was done, over, finished, and people were clapping after what looked like a movie that had been streamed in triple time. It went extremely fast, and I did not keel over, forget where I was, or stumble over my own story. I told the truth that day, and the response was overwhelming. After being individually thanked by twenty-plus people, I took my seat and felt this giant boulder being lifted off my back. Family and personal secrets do keep you sick. Being truthful, sharing from your heart, and honestly telling others about your story help you feel accepted, loved, and less ill. At least that is what I experienced that day, and at every other training that I did for the next three years.

My new position was relatively easy, based on the jobs that I had previously. No problem finding some peers to participate or designing a training program that would be useful. I am very relaxed with most people and could certainly relate to this group who chose treatment over jail. The staff for this Bridge program was dedicated and passionate about their work. We were a good team. I guess that I do have a three-year itch, as it was about that long when I started feeling stressed about my job. I had successfully stopped the ECT treatments, changed medications several times, but was still having difficulty getting a good night's sleep. My job description included twenty-eight hours per week, and I was expectantly working overtime between forty and fifty hours per week and not getting paid for the extra time. Being an overachiever followed me into every job, and this one was no exception. I was not suicidal but very depressed, and I could tell that my brain chemistry was off. Fortunately, my support team, especially my spouse, recognized some telltale symptoms and suggested that I quit the job, take a hiatus, and maybe go for a short hospitalization. I did all three and continued to be on the faculty of the CIT training. Since my story was out there, it was OK to be the person living with a mental illness, and I got involved with several mental health agencies in my spare time. Serving on the Board of the local Mental Health of America did not cut into much of my golf time and satisfied my need to be of service. I had stabilized with my new medication regiment and was sleeping through the night with only three trips out of bed, around 1:13 am, 3:16 am, and 5:20 am every night. *Am I the only one who wakes up on the hour and some minutes or does everyone see seconds on their digital clock?* That sleep cycle is about the same today. If it works, don't fix it.

* * *

It was time to visit my mother and learn more about those islands. Chris and I drove to Charlotte, North Carolina, and climbed on board the flight to Providenciales, which is known as Provo and is the most significant tourist spot in the Turks and Caicos. If you don't know where they are, look them up. We had to. It is approximately 500 miles east of Miami and 100 miles north of Haiti. My mother and brother had successfully developed this island. The resort centered around one of the most beautiful white sand coves in the British West Indies. It was not entirely deserted, but almost. Most of the natives, called "belongers," are from Haiti and make a living with construction or taking tourists caving, fishing, or snorkeling. After landing on the main island, you can take a ferry (that my brother owned) or a flying puddle-jumper that lands on a very bumpy sand runway. Our first visit is worth description.

I had been missing the wild side of my mother, her eccentric personality since I left her house in Switzerland and moved to the States. Not only does she live in exotic places, she takes on fascinating roles that influence all those who come into her company. Let me give an example. Most of the belonger homes on Middle Caicos are concrete brick, unpainted, unfinished, and unkempt. No problem. Dottie, my mother, decides to have a contest. She contacts and contracts with Sherwin Williams to furnish free paint to the island. She orchestrates a contest and offers a monetary prize for any belonger who can paint his house (wild pastels included) and do so within two weeks. The competition begins, and the outcome is still evident today. Wild-pink, fluorescent-yellow, sky-blue, and passionate-purple homes stand proudly. We have no idea who won, but back to our first visit.

By this time, Chris and I had been breeding Labrador Retrievers for twenty years. It is incredibly hard work, pays poorly, and is the most satisfying, rewarding career that I have ever had. In any case, my mother had asked us to bring her a puppy to the islands on our first visit. We chose a six-month-old yellow Labrador to fly down with us. No one expected any problems until we landed in Miami to change planes. We had a two-hour layover and were assured that our puppy would be in the air-conditioned cargo hold. After touch-down in Miami, we taxied up to the gate, and there was an announcement by the flight attendant: "Is anyone traveling with a large dog? If so, please come forward immediately." We had only a puppy, but being super concerned, Chris and I made our way to the front of the plane and conjured up the worst possible situation. We were led out of the plane, down a ramp, and finally, a member of the flight crew told us that our dog, "big dog," had broken out of her crate and was running loose in the cargo hold. The baggage crew was so afraid that no one volunteered to catch the vicious, unclaimed predator. Chris climbed up a ramp, called our puppy, and helped her exit within five minutes. There was applause from the ground crew, and they gave us permission to take the puppy into the terminal. The rest of the flight was uneventful until we had to fly in a small tin can, called a Cessna, to our final destination. We had the plane to ourselves except for a rather stout female belonger who was trying to get back to her home. She was petrified of dogs and would only fly if she got in the seat furthest in the back, and puppy dog rode way up front next to the pilot. Fortunately, the captain was a dog-lover and had no trouble with his new canine copilot.

Safe delivery of the puppy preceded a safe visit with mother and my brother. There were no sibling fights, no mother–daughter altercations, and even Chris had a great time. The island is very flat, built on coral rock, and has views of the Atlantic that are breathtaking. Several coral reefs create a snorkeler's paradise. The local fishing guide is called "Cappie," and he is an interesting character. Born in Haiti, he has been on the island for fourteen years. When he was not taking us fishing, he hunted for conch and guided bone fishermen who came from England to this sacred spot. Nothing is cheap in the islands because every building material, food purchase, and housing supply needs to be imported from the States or England. It is often shipped to Provo, the central tourist attraction town, and ferried out to the other islands, like Middle Caicos. Eventually, a causeway will be built between North Caicos and Middle Caicos. It will improve the transfer of goods and services until any major hurricane washes it away. What a life!

We spent ten days playing backgammon, exploring the local caves, diving on all the reefs, and eating the local fare of lobsters and conch.

Edward had become an excellent general contractor for other tourists who wanted to build there and my mother and sister-in-law, Terri, sold lots and argued about whatever. They did not really fight with each other. They just stayed pissed off at each other and my mother was very bitchy. It was kind of curious and uncomfortable to watch. They continued doing this dance for the next twelve years, and everyone was careful not to get in the middle.

The days went by quickly. The puppy was named Daisy and started following my mother everywhere, which is precisely what she wanted and needed. It felt like I had finally done something agreeable for my mother in bringing her new friend, Daisy, to the island. Both Chris and I got our sunburns and climbed into the Cessna to start our journey home. On this vacation there had been no talk about mental illness, jobs, future trips, grandchildren, or money. It was rather odd. I am not sure what we talked about. Something magical happened. You know when you have a nightmare, and you wake up to discover it was all fantasy and just a bad dream. There is a satisfied sigh of relief, and you feel like you are ready for a new day. I felt refreshed after our trip and all the bad anticipated exchanges with my mother never happened. Mostly, I was grateful that the visit to Middle Caicos did not bring out the worst in me or my mother. The vacation to the islands taught me that as dreadful as my past life had been, especially my relationship with my mother, it was time to get rid of all that baggage and start a fresh new life from a brand-new perspective. After all, I had it good compared to most. It was exciting to see what the future brought our way with or without my family of origin. Who is fooling whom? It really was time to put away the resentments, get on that spiritual journey, and see what I could bring to the world instead of taking away from it. No one was keeping score.

Chapter 12: Practicing an Attitude of Gratitude

Living on a small farm in Appalachian rural America is indeed a divine blessing. With our gorgeous views of the mountains, a small creek running through the rear of our property, and beautiful woods and pastures completely surrounding our home, it is a paradise we call home. Growing up on the ocean with breathtaking views of the dunes, I do occasionally miss the beach. I traded the long stretches of sand for rolling mountains and spectacular sunrises and sunsets. Our house is situated between two national forests and explains the lack of homes or other building structures to be seen. We have six acres of hay in the back, five acres of pasture in the front, and our nearest neighbor is over a thousand feet away. *Why would anyone want to leave this private park?* That is the question that I asked myself when we returned from our island vacation. I was seeing familiar things in a much more gratifying, enlightened way. I needed to hang on to this attitude of gratitude and do a personal inventory immediately. Let's get started.

* * *

This personal audit at this point in my life has nothing to do with having a father or not. It stands alone without blame, fear, or resentment. I need to own up to those old character defects once and for all. A sagacious person, a previous AA sponsor, told me that it was counterproductive to look at my parents' flaws. She suggested that I look at the seven deadly sins: sloth, pride, envy, jealousy, gluttony, lust, and anger. In writing, identify how I relate to this world-renowned list. What are my shortcomings? My sponsor suggested that I look at my assets to balance the ledger sheet and not be too self-deprecating during the process. Liabilities on one side of the ledger and assets on the other. It was an epic task, but I was ready to do it.

The details became very cumbersome, but I stuck with it, and the conclusions were very enlightening. I am not a terrible, selfish individual and I am more giving than most. On the other hand, I can still be an egomaniac with prideful tendencies that get in my way and others'. Most people have not had their personalities dissected like I have or been diagnosed down to their hair type. During this inventory, I realized that being honest with myself as to who I am could be extremely helpful. And heeeere's Janet!

After taking a deep breath and slowly exhaling, I admit that I am my mother's daughter. Owning up to that was a huge step forward. Since I never really knew my father intimately, even after I found him, there was still one parent who kept going in and out of my life and left her genetic footprint all over the place. What did I pick up from my mother? I don't mean physically or intellectually inherit. I am talking more like a sweater that picks up lint. She rubbed off on me, and it was time that I admit the similarities between us and examine the characteristics that separate the two of us. I am sure every adult child engages in this process at some time during their life. We all look at our parents with disappointment from time to time, maybe even disgust. The irony is that too often we become who they are. Thank God that you do not have to like acceptance—you just accept it.

The personal inventory process does take rigorous honesty. So, I am going to tell you my perception of who I am to the best of my ability. Keep in mind that I am describing a person "becoming" and not a finished product.

I watched my mother evolve over the years, and I recognized that what I saw as her faults were in many ways her attributes. This was good for the asset side of my inventory.

When I enter a room, the conversation usually stops, and every individual usually greets me warmly and pulls me into their social circle. When I was drinking, people called this "the life of the party," and now I hear "you light up the room." In fact, in any social situation, I am the one that initiates conversations and keeps them going. My husband says that I have never met a stranger. It is true. I can strike up a discussion with anybody, anywhere, anytime. The introverts that I know often envy this talent and ask how I do it. I do not know the answer, except maybe that I was born that way, and it is very recognizable in my mother. We all acknowledge that there are "doers" and "thinkers." Well, I inherited both genes and almost always inspire others to create meaningful endeavors that transform the current status. I am extremely competitive and have a driving force to be the best in anything. Wanting to be number one often puts me in a leadership role, and I am highly successful in executing the procedure or plan to almost everyone's satisfaction, including my own.

Here is an example. Three years after joining my current church, I was asked to run for President of our congregation. I would have a practice year as President-Elect, serve as President, and then continue to lead as Past President for one more year. It was an awesome responsibility, and I jumped in with both feet for the opportunity to lead. I was hugely successful all three years. Not because of my brilliance, but for the ability to bring the best out of other people, I met the challenge head on. I was able to organize my life and bring others along the same path. Not only create a vision but strategize, so the whole congregation went the best direction possible. Does this sound egotistical? Probably. It is a gift, and I can thank my mother and my father for passing it on to me.

Few people can say they are a born leader, and I am one of them. The challenge is not to get so focused that I have blinders on. You can pay a hefty price in a leadership role and forget how important balance is for you and others, especially those you love. My assets sometimes cross over into my liabilities. When I was younger and working in the world of real estate, my production goals were over the top. I was the best and had many awards to prove it. However, I had no idea of the price that I was paying for that success. My marriage suffered, and my children were becoming orphans. My work life became my identity, and my family life began to disintegrate. Forty years separate my recent church experience from my real estate climb. Today I can tame the dragon and teach him to balance my life with family, friends, church, and travel. It is a process and not an event.

I do have an incredible adventuresome spirit and love to learn new stuff. I use that word because I remain very teachable and my new endeavors are so varied. I do canoe or kayak every week; I am still an avid golfer (can outdrive most men my age); I love to discover new things in my gardens; I love to embrace change in my relationships; and I am pretty eager when it comes to learning something new. This week, my head was wrapped around the current politics (ugh!). I am like a sponge soaking up the procedures for the state legislature and trying to follow a divided national crisis. We can only guess what lies ahead.

* * *

My mother, myself. There are so many similarities. My mother also had a full life and was continually moving locations. Her need for change, any kind of change, was not only recognizable in her life, but in mine. I have described this as running away, seeking a geographical cure, or bailing out on her family. Maybe I have gained a new perspective and do see that her need for adventure and change motivated her actions. Seeking new goals was a good thing.

How many teenagers can say that they captained a forty-two-foot yacht to the Caribbean? It was my mother's keen sense of adventure that sparked this trip and created a sixteen-year-old captain—me.

Recently I was complimented for my ability to organize a dinner and presentation for all the Past Presidents of our church. There were sixty-two on record: several were deceased and some had moved out of the area. Since this had not been done for many years, I was met with an extremely negative attitude by some. "You will never get that group together." "Why would they want to meet anyhow?" "It's too much work." The more criticism that I received, the more challenge I felt. I just wanted to create an evening with all that talent in one room, celebrating and commemorating a job well done. Perseverance is the asset that I am describing, and I have a big dose of it. Do not tell me that it cannot be done. I will persist and make it happen. Again, I did not do this alone. I was able to convince others to help, sell the concept, and the results were fantastic. Thirty-two Past Presidents dined, shared war stories, laughed, and gave valuable insight into the direction the church should go. A good time was had by all.

The last character trait that I would like to take credit for is courage. It is in my genes. It is not something that I was taught in college, and I did not pick it up at the corner market. My mother was very courageous, and she showed me what she knew.

It seems appropriate to talk about humility at this juncture. The Saint Francis of Assisi prayer reminds us to stay right sized. "It is better to be understood rather than to understand. Where there is hatred, let me sow love." And so on. Unveiling my assets and my liabilities demonstrated to me that I have a long way to go in my quest to be a better person. Humility is the cornerstone that I wish to use to build my new life. I am getting better, but I am not there yet. I must keep learning and keep my ego in check. Over the years, I have discovered that I am just not that important and the world does not revolve around me.

There was never a question in my mind, *Are you my mother?* In fact, I am my mother, and I am proud of it. That took years of rebuilding, forgiveness, and lots of acceptance. She died at the age of ninety-five and spent the last seven-and-a-half years of her life in a nursing home with advanced Alzheimer's. No one should have to live like that. I visited my mother almost every week with her favorite Labrador Retriever, Sugar, by my side. The visit always began with me trying to relax her hands. Her fingers were in a vice grip that kept her unable to hold anyone else's hand, specifically mine. I would pull her fingers apart until she could relax them. You could slice the air with tension, partly because I was fearful a nurse would catch me trying to make my mother do something she could not or be someone she was not. I wanted to hold her hand and pretend that she was the nurturing, sensitive, caring mother that she never was. Sometimes it took me eight minutes to fix her fingers so that my hand could hold hers. What was this all about?

I thought of my marriage vows, "Till death does us part, in sickness and in health." Even with her devastating disease, my mother had control, and I begged her to be someone that she could not be. Eventually, I gave up. I let Sugar lick her hands, and I just tried to be present. By bringing the dog, I learned to let go of those sad feelings, visit with other patients, and go to the parking lot less depressed than when I arrived.

I went to see her at the nursing home on a typical Tuesday morning at 10:15. I spent an hour before the visit shoring up my courage, practicing in my mind what I would say, and knowing that this could be the last visit. None of my siblings, Mother's other daughter or two sons, had seen her for years. She was my responsibility, and I owed her my love. I do not know precisely why I felt this huge obligation, but I did. Put the dog in the car, get Sugar some water, make sure that I had her leash, and drive the twenty-two minutes to the assisted-living facility. It was like any other Tuesday. I regretted going but knew that I needed to visit for my sake and hers. I had learned to love her and gave up trying to make my mother someone that she was not. There was a sense of peace, and this visit was different. As soon as we got to her room, Sugar jumped up on her bed and lay across her chest. Sugar knew. We both said goodbye. There were no tears but a profound feeling of sadness to let her go.

There was no funeral, and my daughter made all the obligatory phone calls to those that had long ago taken my mother out of their lives. We decide to do a memorial service in the Turks and Caicos later in the spring. My husband, my daughter, and I visited the local funeral home to select an urn for her ashes. We viewed her body lying in the casket, and she did look at peace. I touched her cheek, and it was freezing. Someone had fixed her hair neatly as she liked it. She was gone.

Instead of an urn, she stayed in a cardboard box which was sealed and certified by the funeral director so that we could fly her ashes to the islands. Even in death, my mother got her way. No big fuss and no false words at the funeral which was organized for the living. There was a big stone patio built over Dragon Cay in the Turks with a statue of the Praying Hands overlooking the sea. That is where we gathered with the local preacher, the schoolteacher, and several belongers that wanted to say a few words about Momma Dottie, which is what they called her. It was interesting that strangers, to me, were able to call her Momma when I never could. I never got past "Mother." My older brother and his wife; my daughter, her husband, and her son; and Chris and I joined the group to say goodbye. The biggest gift that my mother ever gave to me was my "real" father. I was grateful.

Chapter 13: Soaring like an Eagle

This memoir would not be complete without describing the father that was so difficult to find and what he passed on to his daughter, me.

My father was an eagle. He soared above everyone else in everything he did, especially in his career. This part of the story is easy to reconstruct, as he wrote an autobiography that chronicled his life from birth to his death in 1999. A friend of his who had followed his Naval career used a 300-page diary of the Admiral's to coauthor the book. My father gave the biography his blessing before he died.

You know how I felt during his funeral. Isolated, ignored, not welcomed, profoundly sad, and unloved describe the emotional roller coaster that I experienced that day in Arlington cemetery. How did I feel after discovering who he was and hence, his influence on me?

This journey begins with the first letter that I received when I was nineteen and was signed "Love, Daddy." Where do I go from there? Just like my AA sponsor suggested, it is like peeling an onion. There are layers upon layers to be uncovered which reveal different experiences that I had with my father. Most of these were revealed, but who is this man that I can now call "Dad"? First, I referred to him as "Matt" or "the Admiral" and never "Dad."

After dropping out of high school, he enlisted in the Navy when he was sixteen, which was under the required age. No problem. Matt went out in the park adjacent to the recruiting office and found two hobos to forge his parents' signatures. The day he enlisted, he lined up with fellow newbies and was shorter and scrawnier than any of the other men that were in front of the recruiter. The big old bosun's mate was sizing up his recruits and made this statement to Matt: "And how in the hell did a little scrawny thing like you get in here amongst all these grown men?" Through the years the Navy chose to overlook his fraudulent act of the age discrepancy and advanced Matt through post after post until he became a Vice Admiral, a nuclear physicist, and a father of five children (or six).

He was an overachiever and extremely competitive. Sound familiar? It was not until I read his book that I understood the connection between the Admiral and my family. Except for the apparent connection, me.

In 1949, Matt was moving his family from the East Coast to Palo Alto on the West Coast. He spent the Christmas holiday with his two older girls driving cross-country and his wife, and the three younger children would join him after he found a house and got settled. They were on the road and made it to California on New Year's Eve. Matt headed down to the bar and was buying drinks for several young women until his oldest daughters found him and reported to their mother the impropriety. It was shortly after this trip west to California that Matt met my mother. It was a one-night stand, and I was the result. That is how my mother had described the affair. The Admiral talked about chemistry and the love that he had for my mother. I would guess that the event falls somewhere between those two poles.

At this time, my mother was married to Bruce King, a Navy doctor, and they had one son, Edward, who had just turned seven. You will see how the connections to the Admiral do not stop with both being in the Navy.

***

I was born November 25, 1950, in Norfolk, Virginia. My mother and my oldest brother had flown to the East Coast the previous September so my "then-named" father could start a new tour of duty in Norfolk. This father was supposed to join us from California in the spring of 1951. My mother received the devastating news in movie fashion. Two uniformed naval officers showed up at our front door. Dr. Bruce King was dead, and it was their job to inform my family of the loss.

Being a flight surgeon suggested that Bruce liked to fly, and even though I know next to nothing about his naval career, I did confirm this story. February 1951 was the time when the Navy was testing a new airplane, the AJs. After several crashes and mishaps, the plane was being revamped and refitted to accomplish new goals for the Navy. It was supposed to be fast, carry a large payload, and exceed the performance of anything that came before it. Bruce was having lunch with his buddy, Lt. Matt Hollins, and asked if he could go up in the AJ for the fun of it. Matt found him a ride with another pilot that afternoon, and one-half hour off the tarmac, they crashed into the sea.

My mother told me many, many years later that Bruce knew about her affair with Matt and left evidence of that knowledge. There was a life insurance policy signed by Bruce King that named Dottie King, Edward King, and Janet "Hollins" as the beneficiaries. There was no doubt that the different last name was intentional, and I guess Bruce King did get the final word on that matter.

In the Admiral's autobiography, the crash was mentioned in half of a paragraph and was just a blip in Matt's history. He was much too talented and too busy with his naval career to slow down and take responsibility for his other children or me. They might disagree, and I will never know their story or wish to interfere with the connections that each of my half siblings had with their father, the Admiral. I do know he had a brilliant and robust wife who stood by his side and raised a family with little help from her husband. She knew nothing about me, and Matt Hollins wanted to keep it that way. Was Matt distracted from having a relationship with his bastard daughter? Absolutely!

Early in Matt's career, he learned that book-learning was extremely important and would be the key for his ticket up the ladder. After being a high school dropout, he graduated top in his class at the Naval Academy and flying became his passion. Whenever or wherever there was an opportunity to pilot a plane, Matt grabbed it and logged more hours in a cockpit than any of his contemporaries. He kept studying and taking courses on the side to become a nuclear physicist, which opened up a whole new world for him. The Admiral was a pioneer and assisted not only with the creation of the atomic bomb, but his team discovered the best way to carry this weapon to its enemy. During the war, he received numerous commendations and awards for chivalrous acts and courage beyond anyone's expectations.

There was no doubt he was brilliant, and I was able to pass those genes to my three children, three grandsons, and my granddaughter. What else did this ancestry do for me?

* * *

Demanding perfection is a double-edged sword. The favorable consequences are you exceed expectations of others. It puts you in the limelight and makes you eligible for promotions, possible fame, and an exciting life. The downside is a driving force that makes you highly competitive, subject to burnout, and sometimes challenging to be around. Boy, did I inherit that trait! For the Admiral, the results catapulted his career and took him to cutting-edge projects his entire life. Of course, there had to be a payoff. Something had to suffer, and I would say it was, most definitely, his relationship with me.

Tim Russert, an NBC bureau chief once said: "The older I got, the smarter my father seems to get." In my twenties, the absence of a father just plain hurt. There was no one to give me away at my wedding. There was a missing grandfather to introduce to my children. However, in my thirties, it was my incredible drive and persistence to have a better life that saved my a*$ and taught me how to soar. I credit this tenacity and perseverance as a gift from the Admiral.

Since Matt did serve during Calvin Coolidge's presidency, it seems appropriate to share a Coolidge quote: "Nothing in this world can take the place of persistence. Talent will not; nothing is more common than unsuccessful men with talent. Genius will not; unrewarded genius is almost a proverb. Education will not; the world is full of educated derelicts. Persistence and determination alone are omnipotent. The slogan Press On! has solved and always will solve the problems of the human race." This statement was my father's ethos, and he passed it down to his daughter. It served him well, and it continues to help me with my daily life.

Being perfect and doing your best leads to a competitive spirit which also plays out in everyday life. The Admiral was a golfer and started at a young age to beat his father on the links. He finally did lower his score to the best golfer in his family, but that was not good enough. While enjoying the sport, there was always that drive to lower his handicap and work harder to improve his game. The same was true for water polo. When he was at the Naval Academy, it was crucial to make the cuts to be the best and play for the Navy. I never played water polo in my life, but I have been playing golf for thirty years. My claim to fame is that I can outdrive most women and a few of those men that I already mentioned. When I get up on the tee box, it is imperative that I do my absolute best. Anything less is a disappointment. Please understand that I can be out on the golf course playing by myself with no pressure, out for a beautiful sunny day to relax, and my competitive streak kicks in. My mother was competitive, and this might be a curse that I inherited from both my parents.

During one of our rare luncheons that I had with the Admiral, we talked about being "too" competitive. He asked me to elaborate. I shared that a game of croquet with my family could turn bloody. Card games, especially Bridge or Skip Bo, were especially cut-throat and I would usually set the tone by doing everything in my power to win. A friend of mine and I were sharing breakfast with another acquaintance, Lisa, and she referred a massage therapist to both of us that she thought was quite good. I turned to my friend and told her that I needed the massage most, so she should wait and let me have the first appointment. Her response was: "You are too damn competitive. You always have to be first." After telling my father these examples, I expected some words of wisdom that I could live by. My father said: "What's wrong with being first?"

Comparing my father to an eagle is not by mistake. It is very intentional and meant as a compliment. You see, I have come full circle. I am no longer lamenting this complicated story of finding a father. I am genuinely grateful for the ones that I have had. An eagle stands majestically at the top of the tallest tree, surveys the land below with his keen eyesight, uses his broad wings to soar, and remains acutely aware of everything below him.

My father, the Admiral, was a great man and accomplished so much in his lifetime. I realize how fortunate I am to not only have known this wonderful man, but to be "his daughter" and proud of it. My legacy to my children and my grandchildren is rich because of who I am and who I am becoming.

Epilogue

I do not wish my childhood on anyone. I know that the search for my father and the discovery of my family would not have happened if I had not fallen out of the nest. Many people have it so much worse. I am not unique. My journey caused chaos, crisis, and damage to my loved ones. I wish that I could take that back, but I have been taught not to regret the past, nor wish to shut the door on it. Like most, we learn from our experiences, and we discover choices from our mistakes.

All the fatherly needs of feeling safe, protected, wanted, comforted, nurtured, and loved are right here. All my life I have compared my insides with everybody else's outsides and always come up short. I believed everybody else was all "put-together," felt loved, protected, and did not feel needy, vulnerable, or unsafe. It was an easy assumption to make because I never let anyone get close and I kept friends and family at arm's length. It can be a big cruel world if you travel alone always seeking something outside of yourself. It does help, as a young child, to have a knee to sit on, a firm arm around your shoulder or a large hand to hold as you walk down the beach. The persistence, the grit, and the willingness to go forward when going backward might be the easy way out are "my" choices. It is time to turn roadblocks into stepping-stones.

Taking responsibility for my own parenting and being free to make healthy choices is a massive change in my thinking. I awaken to a new idea that I can love the child inside and stop the self-hatred that has dominated fifty years of my life. In this quest to find my father, I found myself, and I like what I have discovered. I am intelligent, attractive, capable, teachable, have self-dignity, self-worth, sobriety, and can stand on my own two feet. I like the quote: "I am woman; let me roar."

Many women and men in this era grow up in families defined in new terms, blended, single-family, gay, raised by grandparents or relatives, adopted, and yes, cloned (in the near future). Families are no longer structured or judged by who the parents happen to be. It is the love that bonds the family and the values that bind the family. Love is the glue that determines the outcomes of happiness or emotional wellness.

Spending half a century and spanning half the globe, I acted frantically at times to locate one relative—my biological father. Just like the little bird in *Are You My Mother?* I looked in many of the wrong places but tirelessly continued the search for my lost father. He was not lost, and I paid a high price until he was found.

Do we do this in other areas of our life? The career that requires the eight-year commitment to a doctoral program, where all other aspects of your life must be put on hold, including family, friends, or other employment, is a good example. The goal is sometimes so focused, it can create a wasteland along its path. There is the young mother who when she was sixteen gave her daughter up for adoption. She is now forty-three and has spent twenty-seven years painstakingly searching for her lost daughter. This mother also has two biological sons, and they have suffered unquestionably and relentlessly through her efforts to locate this other child who is now an independent adult. These real-life accounts go on and on and will continue as we search for "true" meaning and "completion" in our lives. Continuing to look outside of ourselves does not work. I had to learn that the hard way. This life lesson did result in a shattered family that is still putting back the pieces. I paid a hefty price for my search, and my only hope is that what I learned be passed on to others so that they might benefit from my experiences. After all, that is the gift that we are genuinely given in life. We each have the opportunity to freely give to others what has been so freely given to us.

Today, I genuinely do live one day at a time, and I try to stay present and mindful in that special place. I am blessed to be surrounded by my black Labrador, Trooper, and my sweet Labradoodle, Chloe, who give me unconditional love on a regular basis. My devoted husband, Chris, continues to journey with me, support me, love me, and appreciate me for who I am. My son, my daughter, my three grandsons, and my granddaughter bring me incredible joy. All our parents have passed, but our family continues to grow with a new "daughter-in-law" this past year and two new "granddogs." All the promises that people pledged would come true in my life are here, right here in my spirit. My biggest sorrow, the loss of my son David, remains a hole in my heart. It is incredible that twenty-five years after my son's death, the feelings are still raw and ache all the way down through my body. Sometimes I do cry, but most of my emotions about my son continue to stay choked up in my throat. I do not think anyone can fill that hole, but I do try to be thankful for the twenty years of his life that we did share together.

Learning to fly, flying solo, flying straight, and soaring like an eagle have given me the courage to help others and be of service to my community. That is a significant endeavor, but I continue to put one foot in front of another and do the next right thing.

I invite you to do the same.